Cupcakes and Celebrities – Pelican Cove Cozy Mystery Series Book 2

By Leena Clover

This book is a work of fiction. Names, characters, places, organizations and incidents are either products of the author's imagination or used fictitiously. Any resemblance to actual events, places, organizations or persons, living or dead, is entirely coincidental.

First Published – May 8, 2018

Acknowledgements

A big thank you to my readers, friends and family for their continued motivation and support. I couldn't have done this without them.

Chapter 1

Jenny King fidgeted with her organza dress, trying to ignore the stream of sweat trickling down her back. Why had she ever agreed to be a bridesmaid, she moaned to herself. Could you technically be a bridesmaid if you were in your forties? The peach dress she was wearing was supposed to be pretty, but Jenny looked and felt like a giant pumpkin. The May morning was unseasonably hot, the temperatures already soaring above 95 degrees.

"Stop that," Heather muttered, jabbing an elbow in her side.

Heather Morse was one of Jenny's new friends, a young woman she had met when she came to live in the town of Pelican Cove a few months ago. Jenny was at a loose end after her twenty year old marriage ended suddenly. Her aunt Star had summoned her to the remote Virginia island where she lived.

The past few months had been a blur. Jenny had fallen in love with Pelican Cove and the diverse group of women she befriended had made her feel right at home.

"This dress is too tight for me," Jenny complained, giving Heather a nasty look. "I should never have agreed to do this."

"I owe you one," Heather sighed. "Let's just get through the ceremony.

You can change into something more comfortable as soon as they say 'I do'."

Jenny looked around at her luxurious surroundings. Normally, she wouldn't have been able to set foot in the Pelican Cove Country Club. You either needed plenty of money to get in, or a certain bloodline. Jenny had neither. The Country Club catered to the Eastern Shore elite and only the top families of Virginia's Eastern Shore were members.

"She does look gorgeous," Jenny said, spying the radiant bride who stood a few feet away from her.

Crystal Mars was the most sought after star in Hollywood since she had signed a popular reality TV show. She had a couple of movie deals on the table too.

The wedding was supposed to be hush-hush and on the QT, as they said in the business. Crystal was adamant about having a beach wedding with at least five bridesmaids. She had remembered her distant cousin Heather lived on some remote island on the Eastern Shore of Virginia. One look at the Pelican Cove Country Club had sealed the deal for her. A lavish wedding weekend had been planned, with most wedding related activities squeezed into four days.

"That dress!" Heather said enviously. "It's Vera Wang, you know."

Jenny admitted Crystal had been more than generous with her bridesmaids. The dress Jenny wore was a simple sheath of the finest silk, made by some pricey designer. Jenny couldn't find fault with it, other than the fact that it wasn't her size. But that wasn't Crystal's fault. Jenny was filling in for a girl at the last moment. She was just happy to be part of the wedding party.

"Everything looks beautiful," Jenny nodded, looking around her.

Crystal had chosen white and peach roses for her wedding. The lush green grounds of the country club gently sloped toward a white sandy beach. The turquoise blue waves of the Atlantic Ocean pounded against the shore. A wedding arch covered with dozens of tiny roses in white and peach provided a stunning backdrop for the impending ceremony. The path leading up to the arch was laid with a carpet strewn with petals.

"Shouldn't he be here by now?" Heather spoke loudly.

Crystal turned to glare at her.

A shout went up in the small group just then and someone pointed to the sky. Jenny shaded her eyes with her hands and squinted up.

"What's going on, Heather?"

She could barely make out a small plane in the bright blue sky.

"You don't know?" Heather panted. "That's the groom."

"What?" Jenny asked in confusion.

She had been trying hard to hold her

tongue. The bride had walked down the aisle five minutes ago but the groom was nowhere in sight. Jenny had attributed it to some kind of Hollywood quirk.

There was a smattering of applause as something dropped from the plane. The small speck grew in size as it hurtled toward the ground. A cheer went up as a parachute unfurled over the figure.

"That's the groom?" Jenny asked, her jaw hanging open.

"That's the groom alright," Heather said dreamily. "That's Wayne Newman."

She grabbed Jenny's arm and forced her to look up at the sky.

The next few seconds were a blur. A second body dropped out of the plane and plunged toward the ground. It struck the first body and continued racing down. With bated breath, the crowd watched for the second parachute to open. Something shot up in the sky but no canopy opened. Before anyone realized what was happening, the figure crashed into the four tier wedding cake.

Hardly anyone paid attention to the second big thump. Jenny looked up to see a man dressed in a tuxedo rolling on the ground, trying to untangle himself from a colorful parachute.

A scream pierced the air jarring Jenny's senses. It wasn't the only one. A buzz went up as people swore around her.

"She's dead!" someone said unnecessarily, pointing at the body sprawled across the remains of the lavish wedding cake.

It had cost five figures, Jenny remembered Heather telling her. She leaned closer to peer at the unfortunate soul who had just got a free ride to the other world. The girl looked beautiful even in death. Golden blond hair covered her head like a halo. Her deep blue eyes, now lifeless, stared up at the sky. Her svelte body and long limbs indicated she was well over six feet tall. Jenny's eyes popped out when she noticed a large sapphire nestled between the girl's breasts. Her eyes grew larger when she noticed what the girl was wearing.

"Isn't that…" Heather mumbled next to her.

"It's a wedding dress alright," Jenny said grimly. "The exact same dress Crystal Mars is wearing."

"But isn't that couture? I thought they didn't make two of anything?"

Sirens sounded in the distance, and reality set in slowly as people came out of shock. The groom raced up to the body on the ground, still attached to his parachute. His arm hung at an awkward angle and one side of his face was caked with a mixture of grass and blood.

"Bella!" he exclaimed, running a hand through the girl's hair.

"Don't touch her," Jenny sprang forward to caution him. "The police are on their way."

"What was Bella doing on the plane with you?" Crystal Mars asked.

She held the groom's other arm and her face was white with shock.

"I didn't know she was on the plane," the groom wailed.

People around them looked up then, probably trying to spot the plane. It was nowhere to be seen.

"Make way, please," a familiar voice called out and Jenny felt a surge of relief.

Adam Hopkins, the sheriff of Pelican

Cove, emerged through the crowd, followed by a bunch of deputies and law enforcement types. He took one look at the prone body and started clearing a perimeter around it. Crime scene tape went up and a couple of policemen stood on guard.

"Why don't you folks head over to the club house?" Adam ordered. "We will want to take a statement from each of you."

The crowd slowly made way to a pavilion at the end of the grounds. Finally, Adam spared a glance at Jenny.

"Hello Jenny," he said softly. "I didn't expect to see you here."

"Crystal's my cousin," Heather spoke up. "A distant cousin."

"I heard about that," Adam told her.

"One of the bridesmaids pulled out due to a last minute gig," Heather explained. "There was a spot in the wedding party. Crystal wanted Jenny to be part of it."

"Another one of your fans?" Adam asked Jenny, cracking a smile.

"Jenny made cupcakes for the wedding shower," Heather nodded vigorously. "Crystal can't stop raving about them."

"So what happened here? Did you ladies see anything?"

"It was all a blur," Jenny spoke up. "Literally. It all went down in a couple of minutes. One minute we were watching the groom arrive in his parachute, and the next we were staring at that poor girl."

"Do you know who she is?" Adam asked Heather. "Is she one of your relations?"

"Oh no," Heather shook her head. "She wasn't in the wedding party. And I don't think she was on the guest list either."

"Looks like someone decided to crash the wedding," Adam said, scratching his head. "I wonder why."

"Crystal and the groom both seemed to know her," Jenny supplied. "They called her Bella."

"Bella Darling was the girl Crystal replaced on the show," Heather said, snapping her fingers. "She had the lead role first but then they pulled her out and Crystal got the part."

"Bella Darling?" Adam said doubtfully. "That's actually a name?"

"It could be her professional name," Heather explained, "but it's a name nevertheless."

"Just like Crystal Mars, I guess," Jenny shrugged.

"I need to go talk to all the guests," Adam said. "I'll see you ladies later."

He barely leaned on his cane as he walked away.

"Is Adam getting better?" Heather asked Jenny. "He's hardly using his cane now."

"It depends," Jenny said, not wanting to speak on Adam's behalf.

Adam was dealing with a war wound which hadn't quite healed yet. He was in extensive physical therapy and Jenny had seen him popping pain pills quite often. He hobbled around with a stick but lately his condition seemed to be improving.

"Has he asked you out yet?" Heather giggled.

Adam Hopkins and Jenny King had been at odds with each other since they met. But neither could deny the spark between them. Jenny's inquisitive nature did not help. When her aunt had been unjustly accused of a tourist's murder earlier that spring, Jenny had done all she could to help her out. Adam saw it as interfering in police work and he made his opinion clear.

"He doesn't see me that way."

"Are you kidding? Adam Hopkins has the hots for you. We can all see it clearly."

"I don't," Jenny said stoutly.

She secretly had a big crush on Adam but she wasn't ready to admit it yet, not even to the Magnolias, the group of friends who met for tea everyday at the Boardwalk Café.

"I guess we won't be able to sample the wedding brunch now," Heather grumbled. "It's been ages since I had the Eggs Benedict at the Country Club."

"For shame, Heather," Jenny said. "Show some respect."

"We didn't know her," Heather objected. "Why do all these people drop dead in our town?"

Jenny had no answer for that.

Chapter 2

Jenny walked to the café the next morning, taking deep breaths of the fresh morning air. The sun was rising over the Atlantic, painting the sky in tones of pink and orange. She sat on her favorite bench overlooking the ocean and watched the sun come up. This was her special time of the day, a few moments to herself before the day caught up with her. The Boardwalk Café was getting busier as the tourist season ramped up.

"Good Morning!" Petunia Clark greeted her with a fresh cup of coffee.

"How are you, Jenny?"

Petunia's double chins wobbled as she spoke. She had been running the Boardwalk Café for the past twenty five years.

Jenny barely had time to gobble a blueberry muffin before the breakfast rush started. Her favorite customer was first in line.

"Blueberry muffin for you, Captain Charlie?" she asked an old sailor who came to the café for breakfast and lunch.

"What's the world coming to?" Captain Charlie clucked. "I heard a young girl died at that fancy club yesterday."

Jenny spent some time telling Captain

Charlie about the poor dead girl.

"Sounds like some funny business," Captain Charlie said, narrowing his eyes at Jenny. "Are you going to look into it?"

"Oh no! I have enough to do here. See you at lunch, Captain Charlie. I'm making crab salad again."

Jenny flipped her special pancakes, baked trays of muffins and poured endless cups of coffee for the next few hours.

She glanced up at a wall clock when she heard Heather's voice. Heather peeped into the kitchen just then, looking for Jenny.

"Ready for a break?" she smiled.

Jenny had begun to look forward to these mid-morning breaks with her friends. The group of ladies got together at the Boardwalk Café and exchanged gossip and pleasantries over coffee and muffins. Jenny heard the clacking of knitting needles and knew Heather's grandma Betty Sue had accompanied her as usual.

Heather and Betty Sue Morse ran the Bayview Inn on the island. Betty Sue was the fourth generation descendant of James Morse, the first owner and inhabitant of the island. It had been called Morse Isle then.

James Morse of New England travelled south with his wife Caroline and his three children in 1837. He bought the island for $125 and named it Morse

Isle. He built a house for his family on a large tract of land. Fishing provided him with a livelihood, so did floating wrecks. He sent for a friend or two from up north. They came and settled on the island with their families. They in turn invited their friends. Morse Isle soon became a thriving community.

Being a barrier island, it took a battering in the great storm of 1962. Half the island was submerged forever. Most of that land had belonged to the Morse family. A new town emerged in the aftermath of the storm and it was named Pelican Cove.

Betty Sue was a formidable woman in her seventies and her word was law.

"Take a break now, Jenny dear," Petunia ordered.

The ladies sat at their usual table out on the deck overlooking the Atlantic Ocean.

"Where is your aunt today?" Betty Sue asked, pulling some lavender wool over her needles.

Rebecca King or Star, Jenny's aunt, was an artist. Now that the days were warmer, Star spent most of her time painting outdoors, her easel set up on one of the numerous beaches or bluffs across the town.

"I'm coming, Betty Sue," a voice sounded as Star came up the stairs from the beach.

She was dressed in a loose, bright colored kaftan that had been hacked off mid thigh. A couple of paintbrushes poked out of her pockets.

"Stop harassing my niece."

"Who said I was harassing her?" Betty Sue took the bait.

"Where's Molly?" Jenny asked, pulling out a chair for her aunt.

Molly Henderson worked at the local library and was Heather's age. She was another of Jenny's new friends.

Petunia came out with a tray loaded with a fresh pot of coffee and a plate piled high with muffins.

Jenny sniffed at her sweaty armpits and longed for a cold shower.

"I never knew it could get so hot in

Virginia."

"Wait till July," Star said, "or August. You'll have sweat pouring down your eyes."

"Settle down, girls," Petunia twittered. "I want to hear about what happened at the club."

"Me too," Molly, a tall lanky girl with thick Coke-bottle glasses said as she came out on the deck through the café, slightly out of breath. "You've done it again, Jenny."

"What have I done?" Jenny asked, stuffing a piece of muffin in her mouth.

She savored the flavor of the organic vanilla extract she used. She liked to use plenty of berries so they just burst forth in every bite.

"You have all the fun," Molly said petulantly. "I hear you were present when that girl fell from the sky."

"Are you out of your mind, Molly?" Jenny growled. "A poor young girl lost her life. Where's the fun in that?"

"I guess it wasn't fun for the girl," Molly agreed. "So does anyone know what happened?"

"It looked like she jumped down," Heather told the girls. "Now why should she do that? Do you think it was suicide?"

"She was dressed in a wedding gown, wasn't she?" Betty Sue Morse said, pausing her knitting for a moment. "I say she wanted to ruin the wedding."

"Oh yes," Star said, sipping her coffee. "What about the wedding? I suppose those two didn't get married after all."

"Crystal was too worked up," Heather pronounced. "They could have been married inside privately, but she said she wanted to hold off on the wedding."

"What a colossal waste," Petunia declared. "I can't imagine spending an arm and a leg on something and not going ahead with it. Why! I would have fainted from the shock."

"This is just chump change for those people," Heather said. "Crystal makes a lot of money. A lot…"

Adam Hopkins walked up to the café, looking formidable in his uniform.

"Ladies!" he greeted them.

Jenny got up to see what he wanted.

"I have to go the mainland," he told her. "I thought I might get some lunch to go. I will stop at some rest area on the way and eat in my car."

"How about some grilled chicken salad? It's a new recipe I am trying out for the summer. I would like to get your opinion on it."

"Why not?" Adam shrugged. "Anything you make is delicious, Jenny."

"It's on the house," Jenny smiled up at

him. “But you will have to give me your honest feedback.”

“When do I not do that?” Adam laughed.

“So you’ll tell me tonight?”

“I might not be able to make it to the beach.”

Jenny lived with Star in a beach facing house. It was one of the few beaches in Pelican Cove offering a flat stretch of land without any rocks or dunes. Adam Hopkins had a habit of going there for a walk. He had run into Jenny there a few times. She had been out to stretch her legs after dinner. It had become a habit and now they met on the beach by an unspoken arrangement.

"You have a doctor's appointment in the city?" Jenny asked with concern.

"Not this time. I'm going there on official business."

Jenny nodded in understanding.

"This is about that poor girl, isn't it? Has anyone come asking for her? Does she have any family?"

"I can't tell you that, Jenny. Wait till the grapevine catches up though. You'll know soon enough."

"We were talking about her just now. Do you think it was suicide? Or an accident?"

Adam gave her a withering look.

"You're not going to be mixed up in any funny business again, are you?"

Jenny shook her head.

"I've learned my lesson, Adam."

She had narrowly escaped an attempt on her life earlier that year when a killer tried to get rid of her.

"I want to believe you," Adam said, his blue eyes twinkling with mischief. "But something tells me you'll find a way to butt in."

"Are you saying I butt in on purpose?" Jenny asked, her hands on her hips. "I don't even know these people. And we are getting too busy here at the café. I think I will have to give up my mid-morning break soon."

"What about the extra help Petunia was going to hire?"

"We signed a couple of kids on. They start after Memorial Day."

"Is Nick going to be here for the summer?" Adam asked after Jenny's son.

"I haven't talked to him all week," Jenny wailed. "The twins might know more than me."

Adam's twin girls had met Jenny's son and they had hit it off.

"You think the twins call me every day?" Adam sighed. "Sometimes I feel like they barely tolerate me."

"You are pretty cool as a Dad," Jenny

consoled him. "They are just busy, I guess."

"I hope at least some of that time is devoted to studying," Adam snorted. "They might look all cherubic but they are a handful."

"You don't suspect foul play, do you?" Jenny burst out.

"There you go again," Adam sighed. "Stay out of this one, Jenny. Please."

His voice softened as he leaned toward her.

"I don't want to be mad at you."

"Then don't be," Jenny said, suddenly feeling out of breath.

"I have a job to do. Calling out people who interfere is part of it."

"Alright, alright. Message received. Drive safely, okay?"

Adam Hopkins took the bag Jenny handed him. It felt suitably heavy and Adam felt his mouth water as he thought about any extra treats Jenny may have packed for him.

Jenny went out to the deck after Adam left, unaware of the smile that lit up her face.

"When are you going out with him?" Molly asked.

"Come on, Molly," Jenny sighed. "Not that again."

"Adam Hopkins needs a kick in his pants," Molly Sue declared.

Star and Petunia agreed with her.

"I don't see what he's waiting for," Star said. "Jason's going to whisk you away one of these days."

"Speaking of…" Petunia said, tipping her head toward the boardwalk.

An attractive black haired man dressed in a suit walked up the steps of the café.

"Hey Jenny!" he called out. "Good Morning, ladies! What's the latest in Pelican Cove today?"

"What do you think this is, boy?" Betty Sue scowled. "Gossip Central?"

Jason gave her a cheeky smile indicating what he thought. Jason Stone was a lawyer, the only lawyer in Pelican Cove. He was one of the Pioneers, the oldest families on the island. He had moved back to the small town after getting tired of the rat race in the city. He had known Jenny years ago when she spent summers on the island as a teenager. He was as impressed with her now as he had been then. Unlike Adam, he made it very clear how much he liked Jenny.

"Aren't you in court today?" Jenny asked with surprise.

"Just getting back from the mainland," Jason told them. "One of my cases got pushed. I thought I might have an early lunch before I go back to the office.

I've got plenty of work piled up on my desk."

"Jenny will take care of you, dear," Petunia said meekly.

Jason pulled Jenny up to her feet and put an arm around her shoulders. He whispered something in her ear and almost dragged her back toward the kitchen.

"That's a man who means business," Molly said dreamily. "He just takes charge of the situation, doesn't he?"

"Chris should take a page out of his book," Heather said cattily.

Heather had been dating Chris Williams since a long time. Their families approved of the match and were waiting for Chris to pop the question.

"Summer is going to be interesting this year," Betty Sue cackled, gathering her skeins of yarn. "Time to go, Heather."

The little group broke up, everyone going back to their jobs. Petunia walked into the kitchen to find Jason curling a strand of Jenny's hair in his fingers.

"But why not?" Jason was saying. "You gotta eat."

"Only if you let me pay," Jenny said.

"No way, Jenny. I asked you first. And why do you get so hung up on who's paying?"

Jenny liked Jason Stone a lot. He was smart, good looking, gentle and considerate. He wasn't given to sudden bursts of temper like Adam. But unlike Adam, he didn't make her blood boil.

Chapter 3

Jenny hummed a tune to herself as she chopped celery for her crab salad. Chris Williams had come over with five pounds of jumbo lump crab meat from freshly caught Chesapeake crabs.

"People are loving the chocolate cupcakes," Petunia chortled as she came in with an empty tray.

"Should we make a double batch?"

"Not yet," Petunia said. "Let's keep the supply shorter than the demand. That's a great way to spread the word without spending anything extra."

"That's smart, Petunia," Jenny said, her admiration clear in her voice.

"I've been running this café for twenty five years, girl. I picked up a trick or two."

Jenny added chopped celery and sweet peppers to the crab meat. A generous helping of Old Bay seasoning went in along with fresh lemon juice.

"What's happening out there?" she asked curiously as she started mixing the salad gently.

A faint buzz was coming from the café. Heather came in, followed by another girl. Jenny and Petunia couldn't hide their surprise.

"Hello Heather."

"You remember Crystal?"

Jenny gazed a bit enviously at the tall, slim girl who had come in with Heather. Blonde and blue eyed, she was a real life Barbie doll. Almost six feet tall, her gentle curves were outlined in the perfectly cut summer dress she was wearing. Must be a pricey designer label, Jenny guessed correctly. Crystal Mars glowed like a bright star shining in a midnight blue sky.

"What brings you here?" Jenny asked.

She had never imagined a celebrity like Crystal would actually come to the Boardwalk Café.

"Can we talk?" Crystal asked, looking around her.

The expression in her eyes warred with the smile on her lips. Crystal Mars was clearly out of her element.

Jenny looked at Petunia, silently asking her permission. The lunch rush was about to begin.

"Can you fill orders while you talk?"

Jenny quirked her eyebrow at Crystal.

"Do you mind if I make sandwiches while you talk?"

Crystal shrugged.

"This is a busy time for us," Jenny explained.

"That should be fine," Heather said hurriedly.

She pulled out a couple of chairs and pushed Crystal down in one.

“So tell me,” Jenny said, scooping crab salad onto a slice of bread. “What brings you here?”

She added sliced tomato and lettuce and pressed it down with another slice. Placing a toothpick through the center, Jenny placed the sandwich on a tray. They would be flying off the shelves in the next half hour.

“You know what happened yesterday,” Crystal said, rubbing the bridge of her nose.

Jenny realized Crystal was barely holding it together. There was a hint of green below her eyes indicating she hadn’t slept well.

"You mean the girl?" Jenny asked, trying to be delicate.

"The dead girl," Crystal nodded, not wasting any effort on being subtle. "Bella Darling. I want you to find out what happened to her."

"We have a good police force here in Pelican Cove," Jenny said. "They will get to the bottom of this soon."

"The police don't work for me," Crystal dismissed. "I want my own man on the job."

Jenny let the sexist remark slide.

"I'm not a qualified investigator or anything. You can hire a skilled person for this. You are not short on resources."

"I can pay you double your usual fees."

Jenny opened her mouth to protest.

"Triple. Okay, I will give you a ten thousand dollar bonus on top of your expenses."

Jenny rubbed the charm hanging around her neck on a chain. Her son had given her a gold charm for her birthday every year since he turned eight. She had worn them on a bracelet for several years. She had lately strung them on a gold chain that hung around her neck. The charms lay close to her heart and made her feel closer to her son. She had fallen into the habit of rubbing the charms when she was nervous or disturbed.

"It's not about money, Crystal. Tourist

season is coming up. Petunia needs me here at the café."

Jenny belatedly remembered her promise to Adam. He would not be happy to see her meddling in the investigation.

"Do it at your convenience," Crystal pleaded. "I won't be keeping tabs on you."

"Why come to me at all?" Jenny argued.

"Heather told me about that killer you caught last month."

"I was just trying to help my aunt out. She was the prime suspect."

"So help me out this time. Please…"

"What exactly do you expect from me?" Jenny asked.

Petunia came in and Jenny passed the tray full of crab salad sandwiches over to her.

"Wayne is going to be in trouble. I want you to help him, just like you helped your aunt."

Jenny tried to frame a diplomatic reply.

"My aunt was innocent. I knew that 100%. I can't say the same about your husband. I barely know him."

"He's not my husband yet," Crystal hastened to correct her. "We could have been married yesterday. The judge offered to do it after the police finished taking everyone's statement. But I called it off."

"You don't trust him?"

Crystal gave her a pained look.

"I don't know what came over me yesterday. I made a mistake. I should have gone ahead with the ceremony."

"Can't you do it now?"

Crystal massaged her forehead with her fingers. She looked at Heather and sighed dramatically.

"Wayne won't do it now," Heather explained.

"He's sulking!" Crystal cried.

She probably thought she had dibs on being drama queen, Jenny thought to herself.

"He's acting up!" Crystal wailed again. "He's mad at me because I called off the wedding."

"So you're doing this to appease him?"

"I want to show him I care. Hiring you will help me prove that."

"So you want me to fake this?" Jenny asked, outraged.

"I don't care what you do," Crystal dismissed. "Meet a few people, ask a few questions, do your thing."

"What about the truth though?" Jenny asked.

"I don't care. I just want Wayne to stop

whining and say yes so we can tie the knot."

"I don't think I can help you," Jenny said.

She was seething inside. She burst out again, unable to stay quiet.

"So you don't care if your husband had a hand in killing that poor girl?"

"Don't be silly," Crystal said, standing up. "Bella Darling was a two bit actress trying to make it big. Wayne wouldn't give her time of day. He hardly knew her."

"But what if he is tied up in all this?" Jenny asked.

"Then he is. Just get him to sign on the

dotted line."

"That's up to him. I can't convince him to marry you."

"You just play Nancy Drew. Leave the rest to me."

"There won't be any play acting, Crystal. If I do this, it's going to be as real as it gets. I am going to ask tough questions. Any new information I learn will be shared with the police. I'm going to be looking for the truth. So if either you or Wayne or anyone close to you is involved, I won't be able to help you."

"I'm getting a migraine," Crystal moaned. "Why are you making this so difficult?"

Jenny poured a fresh cup of coffee and handed it to Crystal.

"Can I have one of those cupcakes?" Crystal asked hopefully. "It's not like I have to fit into a wedding dress now."

"I think she just fell off the plane," Heather said, taking pity on Crystal.

Crystal began to nod but Heather cut her off.

"But what was she doing there in the first place? You say Wayne doesn't know her?"

"He knew her name," Jenny said, remembering what the groom had said as he stared at the dead girl.

"That could be from a photo," Crystal

said lightly.

She stood up and stared into Jenny's eyes.

"Will you do it?"

"As long as you're ready for the truth, Crystal."

"Whatever. It was probably just a publicity stunt gone wrong."

Crystal snapped her fingers at Heather and walked out, tottering on her four inch heels.

"Of course she wears Louboutins," Jenny muttered to herself.

She didn't get a spare minute for the next couple of hours. Petunia waddled in after the last customer had been served.

"We made record business today. We are going to need a lot more food during the season."

"That's great news for everyone, right?" Jenny asked.

More sandwiches meant more seafood and produce ordered from the local markets and more bread from the bakery. A rising tide lifted all boats, Jenny realized as she noticed the peeling paint in the kitchen. They all needed the boost the tourist season would bring them.

"What was Miss Hollywood doing here?" Petunia asked.

"She wants me to find out what happened to that girl," Jenny explained. "Actually, she just wanted me to pretend to find out what happened. But I told her that's not how I worked."

"Good for you," Petunia cheered. "So are you going to be working on a new mystery?"

"It may be nothing. We don't know how the girl died."

"You will have to talk to the police, huh?"

"I guess so."

Jenny walked to the police station on her way back home. The woman at the desk perked up when she spotted the plate of cupcakes Jenny was carrying.

"You can go right in," she waved, nodding toward a small office.

Adam Hopkins was fiddling with a pill bottle when Jenny went in. She took the bottle from his hand, unscrewed the cap and handed it over.

"Feeling poorly?"

Adam shrugged.

"Nothing new," he said, popping a couple of pills in his mouth.

He took a long sip of water and gave Jenny a questioning glance.

"Dare I ask what brings you here?"

Jenny winced. She could guess what Adam's reaction was going to be.

"Crystal Mars came over. She asked for my help."

"What kind of help?" Adam snapped.

"She wants me to find out what happened to the girl."

"You are doing it again, aren't you?" Adam said, incensed. "I thought we talked about this. Stay out of police business, Jenny."

"I am just going to talk to people, ask a few questions."

"Your few questions almost got you killed. Do you remember that?"

"We don't even know how that poor girl died. Maybe she committed suicide or fell off."

"What interest does Crystal Mars have in all this?"

"Maybe she's just being nice," Jenny said evasively.

She didn't want to tell Adam about the Crystal – Wayne tiff. He would probably laugh at that.

"I don't think this is a good idea."

"I'm not asking your permission," Jenny bristled. She could lose her temper too. "I want to know what you have found out so far."

"How many times have I told you this, Jenny? I can't reveal anything about an ongoing investigation."

"Come on Adam, tell me something.

Did she have a heart attack or something? What happened to Bella Darling?"

Adam slammed a fist on his desk.

"Go away, Jenny."

Someone came in with a file and handed it to Adam.

"The autopsy report just came in. You'll want to see this."

Adam opened the file and flipped through it rapidly. His eyes widened as he read something. He looked up at Jenny and shook his head.

"God help you, Jenny. You have stepped into a big pile of crap."

Chapter 4

"Have you talked to Wayne yet?" Heather asked Jenny the next morning. "Crystal called a few minutes ago."

The Magnolias were assembled on the deck of the Boardwalk Café, enjoying a quick break. Jenny held up her hand as she chewed on her muffin.

"I skipped breakfast today, we are that busy. I'm going to faint if I don't eat anything first."

"I'm going to hold you responsible if anything happens to my Jenny," Star warned Heather. "Why are you sucking up to that Crystal anyway? I thought she was just a distant cousin."

"Barely one," Betty Sue agreed, pulling out a ball of turquoise wool from her knitting bag. "On her mother's side," she said meaningfully, eager to establish Crystal Mars was not related to the Morse family.

"Is she keeping tabs on me already?" Jenny asked spitefully. "I thought she was going to give me a free hand."

"Wayne's talking about leaving. He has a gig in Nashville tomorrow."

Wayne Newman was a country music star. He had met Crystal at some awards function and they had hit it off. They had managed to keep their affair secret from the press.

"He'll have to come back," Jenny shrugged.

"Yooo-hooo…" a familiar voice trilled from the boardwalk.

A collective groan went up among the girls as a familiar figure bustled up the stairs, dragging someone along with her.

"How are you, Barb?" Star asked, trying to be polite.

Betty Sue was rolling her eyes in disdain. She didn't get along with Barb Norton.

"It's a beautiful day, isn't it?" Barb panted. "I have news. Big news."

She tipped her head at the young woman accompanying her. A short, brown haired woman dressed in a formal suit stood next to her. She gave the girls a finger wave and her lips stretched into a smile.

"This is Mandy James, our new consultant. She's going to help us win that Prettiest Town tag."

"Huh?" Betty Sue Morse asked, putting her knitting needles down.

There was very little that made her stop knitting. Heather looked at her grandma in surprise.

"I'm the Chairman of the Prettiest Town Contest Committee," Barb Norton explained. "Don't you remember? We discussed this in the town hall meeting last November."

Star, Petunia and Betty Sue looked at each other.

"That's still happening?" Star asked.

"What do you mean?" Barb sighed. "Of course it is! We filed our application in December. We made the first cut. I corresponded with them while I was in Florida."

Barb Norton spent her winters in Florida with her daughter. She never gave up an opportunity to bring it up.

"What's the first cut?" Heather asked.

"We are small enough," Barb explained. "The contest is for the Prettiest Small Town. Many of the applicants were disqualified because of population density."

"Go on…" Petunia said impatiently.

"Round 2 was a questionnaire," Barb continued. "They wanted to know about our layout, the kind of businesses we had etc. I filled that out."

"Where did you get the information?" Betty Sue asked.

"I keep a lot of records," Barb told her. "I managed. Anyhow, we cleared that step too and Pelican Cove is a finalist in the contest."

"Sounds good, Barb," Jenny said eagerly.

Barb put a hand on her hip and glared

at Betty Sue.

"You might show a bit more enthusiasm. Pelican Cove could be the Prettiest Small Town in the country. It's a big honor."

"We are all ecstatic, dear," Petunia consoled. "What happens now? How do we win this prize?"

"The judging committee will visit all the finalists. They will be here, in Pelican Cove, for the final inspection. We have a month to get ready."

"Get ready for what?"

"For the judging of course. We need to put our best foot forward, look our best. That's where Mandy comes in."

“What’s she going to do?” Betty Sue asked imperiously.

“Mandy’s going to make sure we look our best,” Barb explained. “The town hired her as an image consultant. She’s going to spruce up Main Street.”

“We don’t need to pay big bucks for that,” Betty Sue spat.

“Mandy has hands-on experience,” Barb explained. “She helped a small Kentucky town win Greenest Town. And she helped another town in Colorado win Most Pet Friendly Town.”

“Is that true?” Betty Sue asked.

Mandy nodded and preened a bit. “It’s what I do.”

"So what, you're going to tell us which building needs a lick of paint?" Star asked.

"At the very least," Mandy nodded. "I make a basic study of the conditions, do a gap analysis and come up with an action plan for what needs to be done. Then I coordinate and make it happen."

"Is a month going to be enough time?" Heather asked.

"It's a challenge alright," Mandy James told them. "Most towns hire me well in advance. I need at least three months to execute a systematic overhaul. I will have to put you on fast track."

"Sounds like a lot of mumbo jumbo to me," Betty Sue growled.

"I will make Pelican Cove sparkle like new. You will hardly recognize it."

"We like our town just the way it is, thank you very much," Star said.

"No one's asking your opinion," Barb snapped. "As the committee chairman, I make all the decisions. And I am giving Mandy carte blanche."

"Where is she going to stay?" Heather asked a practical question.

"At your inn, of course," Barb shot back. "You already have her reservation."

"We do?"

"It's under E. James," Mandy spoke up. "Edith is my middle name."

"Do you use it often?" Jenny piped up.

"I'm flying under the radar, you see," Mandy explained. "There's a town in New Hampshire and another in Idaho who want to sign me on. But Pelican Cove looks the best on paper. I think you guys are the strongest contender."

"We are not the richest town though," Betty Sue said, narrowing her eyes.

"I found that out myself," Mandy laughed. "Money isn't everything. I like to win."

"You're pretty confident," Star muttered.

"I have a proven track record," Mandy nodded. "I'm pretty sure I can help you win. Plus, I have never lived on an island."

"Hardly that," Star shot her down. "The new bridge takes you across in ten minutes."

The new bridge Star mentioned had been built in 1970. Star had crossed that bridge to come to Pelican Cove. She had never left.

"Aren't you going to welcome Mandy?" Barb said, widening her eyes meaningfully.

The girls hesitated for a second and then chorused together.

"Can I get you anything, dear?" Petunia asked finally.

"I hope you are as excited about this

contest as Barb. She has assured me everyone in Pelican Cove will pitch in and do their bit. It's a group effort, you see. We are only as strong as our weakest link. You don't want to be that link."

Mandy went on like that for five minutes. The women on the deck began losing their patience. Barb pulled Mandy's arm and gave her a silent nod.

"Let's go. The seafood market is next."

"What's Barb got us into this time?" Betty Sue complained as soon as the women went out of sight. "Prettiest Town indeed."

"Do you deny Pelican Cove is pretty?" Jenny asked her.

"I know that, Jenny, but that's not the kind of pretty Miss Main Street is talking about. You'll see."

"It's all going to be a big waste of time," Star agreed, getting up to leave. "I gotta go now. Have a painting due tomorrow."

That set the others off.

"Where's Molly today?" Jenny wondered.

"One of her coworkers is home sick," Heather explained. "She had to pitch in and watch the front desk."

"What did that Hopkins boy say about the girl?" Betty Sue asked.

"The same thing he always says. He

can't tell me anything about an ongoing case."

"Did he tell you how Bella died?"

"She died from the fall," Jenny said. "The question is, how or why did she fall. And what was she doing up there in that plane anyway."

"Is that all you have to find out?"

"That's just the beginning, Heather. You remember what she was wearing? I have a strong hunch Crystal is going to be involved in some way."

"You're being biased," Heather protested. "You haven't even talked to her yet."

"The way I see it," Jenny said, "the girl

Bella either jumped herself or she was pushed. If she jumped herself, why didn't her chute open? You remember she had one attached to her back. So she either didn't open it or couldn't open it. Or she opened it and something went wrong."

"Stop!" Betty Sue cried. "You're making my head spin."

"Do you think she sneaked onto that plane?" Heather asked.

"I'm going to find out," Jenny said grimly. "What about you, Heather? Are you going to be my wing woman like last time? Or are you going to stick by Crystal?"

"I'm not taking any sides," Heather rushed to clarify. "I can go along with you if you need me, Jenny."

"What about Chris?" Jenny asked. "What does he feel about all this?"

Chris had been Heather's date for the wedding. Although he hadn't had a front row seat to the tragedy, he had been present in the crowd when the girl dropped from the sky.

"Chris is not too crazy about these Hollywood types. He thinks it's all a big publicity stunt."

Jenny shuddered at the thought.

"That's a possible motive, I guess."

"He wants me to stay away from Crystal."

“You might want to listen to that boy, Heather,” Betty Sue ordained. “He’s saying something smart for a change.”

Betty Sue Morse had grown old waiting for Heather to tie the knot with Chris. She was losing her patience with them. Chris had been experiencing her disapproval quite a lot lately.

“Crystal doesn’t know anyone here,” Heather said stoutly. “I’m just trying to show some support.”

“Be careful about that, Heather,” Jenny warned. “You don’t want to be aiding a criminal.”

“You were right there when Bella dropped from the sky,” Heather objected. “Crystal was standing four feet away from us. She’s innocent.”

"Surely you're not that naïve?" Jenny asked. "She could have hired someone for the job."

"Prove it," Heather said. "If Crystal had a hand in this, I will be the first to call the police."

Jenny felt relieved. Heather was so dazzled by the glamour surrounding Crystal Mars, Jenny wondered if she had gone over to the dark side.

Jenny went into the kitchen and started grilling chicken for her salad. Adam had given her two thumbs up for her new salad recipe. Now she hoped the residents of Pelican Cove felt the same. She was trying to come up with a lighter menu for the summer, one that didn't use mayo so it wouldn't spoil in the sun.

"You are wanted outside," Petunia told her.

Adam was standing at the counter, trying to choose between a cookie and a chocolate cupcake.

"How are you, Jenny?" he asked. "Got any more of that new chicken salad?"

"I'm mixing a fresh batch," Jenny told him. "Any more news on Bella?"

"Some, but nothing I can tell you yet."

"Did she have any family?"

Adam gave in.

"Her next of kin will be arriving tomorrow."

"See, that wasn't so difficult."

"Did you meet Mandy James?" he asked.

"Barb Norton brought her around earlier. How do you know her?"

"The police station is situated in a heritage building. I guess we lend a hand in making Pelican Cove pretty."

"She's going to have some pointers for you too then? This will be fun."

Adam rolled his eyes.

"We are too busy already. We don't have time for this frippery."

"Try telling that to Barb. She's in it to win it."

They giggled like naughty high school

kids. Jenny felt right at home, trading town gossip with Adam. She liked this fun side of him. It wouldn't be too long before he was back breathing fire at her though.

Chapter 5

Jenny put her feet up on a chair after another tiring day at the café. She couldn't wait to get some extra help. She just hoped the kids Petunia had hired would have good work ethics and a strong back.

"You can go on home if you want, Jenny," Petunia said. "I can clean up around here."

Jenny swallowed the crab salad sandwich she was eating. She was so tired she could barely taste anything.

"I have to go to the country club to meet Crystal's mother."

"Why didn't you ask her to come here?"

"I have been summoned, Petunia. The queen wants me to go to her castle."

"Hmmm…"

"I should be happy I get to go to the country club I guess."

"Is it really that fancy?" Petunia asked.

Jenny nodded.

Heather stuck her head in through the kitchen door.

"Ready to go, Jenny?" she chirped.

"What is Crystal's mother like?" Jenny asked Heather as they drove to the club.

"I haven't talked to her much. She's a bit intimidating."

"How do you know Crystal so well but don't know her mother much?"

"I barely knew Crystal," Heather began. "I met her at college in my senior year. That's when we found out we were cousins. She dropped out after her first semester though."

"So she's your age?"

"Oh no! She's three or four years younger than me."

"So she's in her thirties too?"

"It's a big secret. She's supposed to be 25."

Jenny thought of the ravishing Crystal Mars, her unlined face and toned body.

"She can carry it off easily."

"It means a lot to these Hollywood types, I guess," Heather mused. "Crystal's flipping out because she turned thirty last month."

"Is that why she's so eager to get hitched to this Wayne guy?"

"Crystal says she was supposed to have at least one marriage under her belt by thirty."

Jenny shook her head, marveling at how people in certain walks of life functioned.

"It's a different life, huh?"

They reached the club soon after and Heather directed her to a small bungalow at one end. A maid wearing the club's uniform ushered them inside to a sun room.

Jenny spotted the resemblance as soon as she spied the woman seated in an armchair. She didn't have Crystal's height but Jenny felt the same blue eyes trained on her.

"Thank you for coming," the woman said primly. "You are the girl my Crystal has been talking about?"

"I was in the wedding party, Mrs. Mars," Jenny reminded her. "I catered your daughter's wedding shower a few days ago."

"Ah, yes, that was you."

Heather had been cowering behind Jenny all this time. The woman ignored her.

"I'm glad you got in touch, Mrs. Mars," Jenny said. "I wanted to talk to you anyway."

"You can call me Kathy," the woman said. "Now tell me when you are going to wrap up all this nonsense?"

Jenny was speechless.

"Err, may I ask what you are referring to?"

"This nonsense about Bella Darling, of course. Just do whatever Crystal wants you to do so we can head home to L.A."

"You live in Los Angeles too?"

"Of course I do. I am Crystal's manager. She has a very tight schedule. I have to make sure she gets her workouts in, eats according to her diet plan, sleeps on time. Hell, I even make sure she poops on time."

"You must know most of the people she meets then?"

Kathy shrugged. Her expression told Jenny she was stating the obvious.

"Did you know Bella Darling?"

"I did not. Neither did Crystal."

"But she recognized Bella right away when she dropped down on the wedding cake."

"She must have seen her in a magazine or something."

"Bella was quite famous then?"

"She was in some big scandal a few months ago. That's a different kind of famous."

Kathy's mouth had twisted in a sneer as she spoke about Bella.

"So you didn't know her personally but you knew of her?"

"Well, if you want to nitpick…"

"I'm just trying to get a clear picture here."

"What was she doing here, ruining my daughter's wedding? That's what I want to know."

"We'll find that out eventually," Jenny assured her. "What about Wayne, your son-in-law?"

Kathy looked triumphant when she heard Wayne's name.

"Isn't he hot? Crystal couldn't have picked a better man."

"Wayne Newman is hot alright," Heather spoke up.

Kathy ignored her again.

"Did Wayne know Bella?" Jenny asked.

"I'm sure he didn't."

"But she was on the plane with him. Surely he must have known that."

"I think she was a stowaway," Kathy declared. "Wayne had no idea she was up there with him."

"Did he tell you that?"

"He didn't have to. I trust him."

"So what do you think happened?" Jenny pressed.

"She tried to pull a stunt and it failed. Sounds like the work of a deranged fan."

"You are saying there was a third

person up there with them?"

"Someone had to have pushed her."

"You really believe that, Mrs. Mars?"

Kathy folded her hands and stared back at Jenny.

"Yes. Now when are you going to wrap this up? You can tell Crystal some fan pushed the girl. End of story."

"That's not how this works," Jenny said, rubbing a gold horseshoe that hung on her chain. "I will talk to all the people involved, try to match their stories. Then I will try to find out what really happened."

"That's what the police do."

"Right…"

"I thought you were playing along for the fat check Crystal promised you."

"Jenny's not like that," Heather said indignantly. "Why would you think that?"

"Is there anything you want to add, Kathy?" Jenny asked. "Do you suspect anyone?"

"Not really," Kathy said. "Like I said, I barely knew the girl."

"You said you didn't know her at all before," Jenny pointed out. "Which is it really?"

"I didn't know her, okay?" Kathy snapped suddenly. "You are such a pest."

She clapped her hands and called out to the maid.

"Show these people out," she commanded.

Jenny turned back to look at the older woman as they left the room. She was staring back at them, her eyes narrowed and full of fury.

"That was weird," Heather said as they got into the car.

"What's she have against you?" Jenny asked her. "I'm sorry, Heather. I didn't know she was going to act like this."

"She's just throwing her weight around. She never gets to be in the limelight, you know. She's backstage all the time."

"That doesn't excuse her rude behavior."

"She wanted a big Hollywood wedding for Crystal. She hates that she had to come to Pelican Cove. She holds me responsible."

"Surely that was Crystal's decision?"

Heather nodded.

"The wedding is hush-hush, or it was supposed to be. I doubt they will be able to stay below the radar once the news of Bella's death gets out though."

"Crystal looks hungry for publicity," Jenny mused. "Why did she want a quiet wedding?"

"It had to do with their show. Crystal's the star of this new reality show, see? It's like a mashup of a few popular shows. A bunch of girls tackle an obstacle course through an Amazon jungle during the day and the winner gets a date with the guy. The guy chooses a bride out of the finalists."

"And Crystal is one of those girls?"

"She is. And she's going to win."

"Wait a minute. How do you know she will win?"

"That's the way these shows work. They already decide who the winner is going to be. Everything is scripted."

"And Crystal marries this guy on screen? Is it a fake marriage?"

"That's the funny thing. The guy is Wayne Newman. He has to look like the most eligible bachelor."

"Hence the secret wedding!" Jenny connected the dots.

"That's what I gathered from bits and pieces I overheard."

"What's the rush? Couldn't they get married on the show?"

"That's a question for Crystal."

Jenny dropped Heather off at the inn and went home. Star was sitting on the porch, sipping a glass of iced tea.

"It's getting too hot," she observed. "I made dinner."

"Do I have time for a shower?" Jenny asked her.

She put on an old tank top and a fresh pair of shorts. Star had grilled some sea bass and made a green salad.

"Any news on that poor girl?" Star asked as they began eating.

Jenny shook her head.

"Adam hasn't given up anything yet. I met Crystal's mom today. She's a cold fish."

"What else do you expect from these Hollywood types?" Star snorted.

"She's lying through her teeth, Aunt."

"Oh?"

"First she said she didn't know Bella at all. Then she said she barely knew her. She's definitely hiding something."

"Where was she when all this happened?"

"She was standing right there, a few feet away from me."

"She couldn't be involved, in that case."

"At least not directly," Jenny conceded. "That's going to be a big problem actually. Everyone other than Wayne, the groom, was standing right there. Plenty of people will vouch for them. Unless they paid someone else to do the deed, they didn't have any opportunity to commit this crime."

"Did the poor girl have any family?"

"Don't know," Jenny said, trying to remember something Adam had said.

"This looks like a tough one. Make sure you watch over your shoulder, Jenny. I don't want you putting yourself in danger."

"Do you think I should drop the whole thing?"

"Why are you doing it, sweetie? Do you feel any obligation to Crystal?"

Jenny laughed nervously.

"Just because she made me a bridesmaid?"

Star didn't say anything.

"Last time, I was trying to pull you out of trouble. I would have done it whatever the cost."

"I know that, and I'm grateful."

"Now I'm doing it because it seems like the right thing to do. And I don't see anyone else standing up for that poor girl."

"You're smarter than most people. I have no doubt you are going to crack this wide open."

"I wish I was that confident," Jenny muttered.

She watched TV with her aunt for a while and stepped out for her walk. The air was perfumed with a familiar scent of roses and gardenias. The house next to her lit up like a Christmas tree after she walked a few steps, set off by the motion detectors. Jenny looked up longingly at the three storey house that sat empty next to her aunt's little cottage. Seaview was the stuff of dreams. She imagined herself standing on the little balcony overlooking the ocean, wrapped in a pair of strong arms. She just wasn't sure who those arms belonged to.

A bark sounded in the distance and a large hairy body leaped through the air and almost struck her down.

"Tank! You little beast!"

She kissed the yellow Labrador on his head and scratched him under his ears. His tongue wagged as he ran in circles around Jenny.

"Where is he?" Jenny whispered in Tank's ear.

"Stop bothering her, Tank!" Adam's voice boomed as he came up to Jenny.

"You know I don't mind him," Jenny said, holding Tank's collar in her hand. "Long day?"

Adam rubbed his eyes and sighed.

"I'm trying to go easy on the pain pills."

His distressed expression told Jenny it was taking a toll.

"You're hardly leaning on the cane now."

"You noticed that," Adam stuttered.

"Of course I did. You'll be walking without it soon. Not that I care. I don't mind either way. It's just…"

Jenny realized she was bumbling like an idiot. She stopped and looked at Adam. He was looking at her with an intense expression.

They both laughed nervously.

"I used crutches for a long time," Adam told her. "Then this cane."

"Will it be odd to walk without it?" Jenny asked.

"Yes," Adam nodded. A hopeful smile spread across his face. "I can't wait."

Chapter 6

A group of nubile young girls trooped into the Boardwalk Café. The sun had barely risen a foot over the horizon. Jenny had just finished serving Captain Charlie. He was usually one of their first customers of the day.

The girls wanted to sit out on the deck. They waved at Jenny as they went out. She recognized them from the wedding party. They were Crystal's bridesmaids.

"We stayed up all night drinking champagne and watching movies," one girl tittered. "We are so hungry! We thought we'd come check out your place."

"I'm starving!" another one of them added. "What can you get us for breakfast?"

They all looked like clones of each other, tall, perfectly sculpted and tow headed. Jenny got to work in the kitchen making crab omelets. It was another summer recipe she was trying to perfect.

"Can we get mimosas?" one girl piped up.

"Sorry, we don't serve alcohol," Jenny said with a grimace. "I can get you fresh coffee."

Petunia brought over a basket of warm muffins and the girls shifted their attention to the food. One of the girls got up after a few minutes and walked to the kitchen.

Jenny looked up as she flipped an omelet on the café's grill.

"These muffins are delish," the girl said, picking tiny pieces from one she held in her hand. "Do you make them from scratch?"

"Of course," Jenny smiled. "Everything we cook here is made from scratch. It's my own recipe."

"You're a great cook."

Jenny was trying hard to remember the girl's name. It was something exotic.

"I'm Rainbow," the girl offered.

"Oh yeah…" Jenny's face cleared. "I'm glad ya'll came here today."

She didn't know what else to say.

"I heard you're going to find out who killed Bella?"

"I'm not sure someone killed her," Jenny said nervously. "Maybe she just fell off the plane."

"Not Bella."

"Did you know her?"

"I guess."

"Were you surprised to see her?"

"It was a shock! Who would've thunk,

huh?"

"She seemed quite young."

"She was. We are all about the same age. In our twenties, you know…"

The girl paused when she said that.

"Bella was the youngest, barely twenty two."

Jenny thought of her college going son.

"That's awfully young."

Rainbow's eyes filled up.

"She deserves justice, you know."

"I agree. I am going to try and get to the bottom of it."

Another girl came up and dragged Rainbow back to their table. Jenny could hear their noisy talk as she plated their food. Bella Darling would never have breakfast with her friends again.

The girls lingered over their meal, chatting nonstop. They were still there when the Magnolias began to trickle in one by one.

"Who's hogging our table?" Betty Sue Morse grumbled, pulling her knitting needles out of her bag.

Heather emitted a cry as she recognized them.

"They're from the bridal party," she squealed and went out to greet them.

Rainbow turned around and looked at

Jenny. There was a question in her eyes but she didn't say anything. Jenny wondered what the girl wanted from her.

Jenny was worked off her feet for the rest of the day. She walked over to the police station on her way home, hoping to pick Adam's brain again.

Adam Hopkins sat in his office with his bum leg propped up on a chair. Experience told Jenny he was going to be in a bad mood.

"Howdy!" she greeted him cheerfully.

"What do you want?" he snapped.

"What's the latest on Bella Darling?" Jenny thought it best to cut to the chase.

Adam's expression told her she was being a pain in the neck.

"We are getting ready to release a statement. That is the only reason I am going to tell you this."

Jenny sat down with a thump, eager to hear what was coming.

"The victim, Bella Darling, died from the impact. She was carrying two parachutes. Both of them had been messed with."

"What?" Jenny cried out. "That means…"

"This is a murder investigation."

"What do you mean, messed with?"

"Her main parachute had been slashed. The backup parachute she was carrying had been turned off."

"Why would someone do that?"

"That's what we have to find out."

"What about her family? Has anyone come to claim her?"

"She was married. Her husband should be arriving soon."

"She was barely 22," Jenny whispered.

"How do you know that?" Adam asked sharply.

"One of the bridesmaids mentioned it."

Jenny spent a few minutes processing what Adam had told her.

"Why was she wearing a wedding dress?" Jenny asked Adam. "And what about that giant sapphire around her neck? Was it real?"

"It was real alright. It's valued at some ridiculous price, over a hundred thousand dollars."

Jenny let out a gasp.

"That much?"

"The wedding dress, the sapphire, it's all part of the puzzle. I guess it's safe to say she wanted to disrupt Crystal's wedding."

"So it was a publicity stunt after all."

"Whatever it was, it went horribly wrong," Adam sighed. "It was the last thing the poor girl did in her life."

"Who's your main suspect?"

"I'm not going to tell you that, Jenny."

"Isn't the spouse the most obvious pick?"

"We will have to establish his whereabouts at the time the crime occurred. We don't know anything about him at this point."

"What about Wayne Newman? He was on that plane too."

"I think everyone knows that, Jenny."

"That makes him the most obvious suspect. Surely he's not that foolish."

"We are still questioning him."

“What about Crystal and the other guests?”

“We will be talking to everyone. That includes you since you were present at the scene of the crime.”

“Just say when, Adam. I hope you solve this case as soon as possible. That poor girl needs justice.”

“We’ll do fine if people stop meddling and let us do our job.”

“Some people welcome extra help.”

Adam refused to take the bait.

“I hear Mandy James is hard at it. She’s going to put you to work soon. Why not leave the detecting to the police?”

"Don't worry about me, Adam. I can multitask."

"You're a stubborn woman, Jenny."

"I've been called worse," Jenny laughed.

She pushed her chair back although she was reluctant to leave. Adam looked up at her.

"How about grabbing a bite at Ethan's? The catch must be coming in now."

Ethan Hopkins was Adam's brother. He had a fish shack in town, famous for serving the best fried seafood on the coast.

"Sorry, can't," Jenny said. "Jason's taking me to dinner."

"Of course he is," Adam mumbled, curling his fists under the table.

"Can I take a rain check?" Jenny asked. "We can go to Ethan's later this week."

"We'll see," Adam said evasively. "I'm pretty tied up for the next few days. I do have a murder to solve."

Jenny's face fell. Adam realized he had been nasty on purpose. He almost apologized but something held him back. He didn't want to force Jenny's hand.

Jenny walked home with an empty feeling in her heart. Had Adam been trying to say something?

Jason Stone arrived at Jenny's house in his luxury sedan an hour later. Jenny was ready, wearing a new summer dress she had ordered online.

"Hello, pretty lady!" Jason whistled, offering his arm.

Jenny grabbed it and waved goodbye to her aunt. Jason always made her smile. Unlike Adam, he wasn't the brooding type. Jenny told herself to forget about Adam Hopkins for the rest of the evening.

"Where are we going tonight?" she asked.

Jason knew a lot of good restaurants up and down the coast of the Eastern Shore. He took Jenny to a new place every time.

"You like Mexican, don't you?"

Jenny fiddled with the radio, trying to tune in to a jazz station.

Jason regaled her with something funny he had read on the Internet. The sun was setting as they reached the restaurant, an unassuming place in a strip mall.

"Wait till you taste their fish tacos," Jason crowed.

The server brought over a basket of fresh fried tortilla chips with red and green salsa.

"So you're serious about this girl, huh?" Jason asked.

Jenny guessed he was referring to Bella.

"I just spoke with Adam. They have

confirmed it was foul play."

"Be careful, Jenny," Jason said, taking her hand in his. "I don't want you to get hurt."

"Star's already warned me to watch my back," she muttered. "Adam thinks I am crazy to do this. And now you…"

"We care about you," Jason said with emotion. "I don't know how I got along without you."

"Aren't you exaggerating?" she asked in surprise.

"Of course I am," Jason said with a laugh. "But honestly, I am glad you came to Pelican Cove."

"I didn't have much of a choice, Jason.

You know my husband kicked me out of my home."

"You have a choice now," Jason said.

Jenny's divorce settlement had come through a few days ago. She had the means to live wherever she wanted now. Jason was one of the few people who knew that.

"Pelican Cove feels like home now. I don't want to go anywhere else."

"Not even to some exotic tropical island?" Jason teased.

"I have my exotic island right here."

The tacos came and Jenny gorged on them with relish.

"This red cabbage slaw is so yummy. I should try making this at the café."

"I may need to have a powwow with you," Jason confided after they ordered dessert. "I have been approached by someone connected to Bella Darling."

"Did Crystal or Wayne hire you?"

"I can't say, yet."

"I would love to pool our resources. You can probably get more out of the cops because of your legal status."

"You can count on my assistance, Jenny."

Jenny shared Adam's information with Jason.

"So that's why her chute didn't open!" Jason shuddered.

"Have you ever been sky diving?"

"Once, and that was enough for me. I can't imagine people pay to have that experience."

"Do you think Bella was a good person?" Jenny mused. "Why did she want to disrupt Crystal's wedding?"

"Professional rivalry?"

"Crystal says she didn't know Bella."

"Doesn't everyone know everyone nowadays?" Jason questioned. "They talk to each other on social media."

"Is that the same as knowing a

person?"

"Nick might have a better answer for that, Jenny. We are the wrong generation."

"Crystal's mother lied about knowing Bella. So I guess Crystal could be lying too."

"I missed seeing you in your bridesmaid's dress. Rumor has it you looked prettier than those twenty year olds."

Jenny whooped with laughter.

"Jason Stone, are you trying to flirt with me?"

"Who says I am just trying?"

They stopped in another seaside town and went for a walk on the beach.

"I might have some good news for you soon," Jason said, taking her arm.

"You mean…?"

Jason nodded. Jenny had put in an offer for Seaview, the property adjoining her aunt's house. It had passed over to some distant heir who had shown no interest in it for years. Jenny was confident they could complete the transaction without any problems.

"Your offer is very generous, against my particular advice. That old house is crumbling. You will have to spend a packet on fixing it up."

"Don't be a naysayer. It's going to be fine."

"I hope you're right, Jenny."

Jason dropped her home after that. Jenny sat outside on the porch, watching the waves batter the shore. The whitecaps gleamed in the dark and a gibbous moon rose over the water.

Jenny tried to picture the last few moments of Bella Darling's life. Did she have time to panic before she hit the ground?

Chapter 7

Jenny was dragging her feet at the café the next day. She had stayed out on the porch until midnight, questioning some recent choices she had made in life. She had tossed and turned for hours after she went to bed. When her alarm went off at 5 AM, she was just falling asleep.

The phone in the kitchen rang insistently. Petunia finally answered it when she went in with an empty tray.

"It's for you," she told Jenny.

"Who could it be?"

"Heather!" Petunia mouthed as she handed over the old fashioned handset to Jenny.

"Hi Heather! Aren't you coming over for coffee today?"

"Jenny, can you spare some time?"

"We are rushed off our feet, Heather. You know things are getting insane here as the season ramps up."

"Wayne's here," Heather whispered. "He's asking for you."

"What does he want?"

"He won't say. He says he will only talk to you."

"Why didn't he come here then?"

"It's the crowd at the café. He doesn't want to be recognized."

"He'll have to wait."

Heather giggled and hung up. Jenny felt pulled in many directions. She decided to curb her irritation and start preparing lunch.

"Do you want to go over to Heather's?" Petunia asked. "Why don't you go there and send her over? I am fine as long as I have someone watching the cash register."

"He can wait," Jenny said firmly. "I'm going to start on the salad."

Jenny tossed the salad, made a platter of sandwiches and frosted her special cupcakes. Only then did she allow herself a break. She gulped some tepid coffee and sat down with a thud.

"I guess you should go over now," Petunia said.

"Okay, okay, I'm leaving!"

Betty Sue, Star and Molly were on the deck out back, catching up on the town gossip. Heather had stayed back at her inn to keep Wayne company.

A salty breeze coming off the ocean ruffled Jenny's hair as she walked to Heather's inn. It was a bright and sunny day in May and summer had definitely arrived in Pelican Cove.

"Finally!" Heather rolled her eyes when she saw Jenny. "I've been wracking my brains trying to make small talk."

Wayne Newman sat sprawled on Betty Sue's Victorian sofa, tapping his foot impatiently. He wore a cowboy hat and a plaid shirt with jeans that appeared plastered to his body. He was shorter than Crystal but his V shaped torso and washboard abs meant he paid equal attention to his appearance.

Jenny noticed a bandage on his left arm. He must have injured himself during his landing.

"Howdy Ma'am!" he said, standing up. "Can you spare a few minutes for me?"

"What can I do for you, Mr. Newman?"

"Call me Wayne. Crystal said she hired a detective."

Jenny instantly disliked his wheedling tone.

"I'm no detective. I already told your wife that."

"She's not my wife yet," Wayne whined. "She won't marry me."

Jenny thought back to what Crystal had said. What was wrong with these Hollywood people? The lies came easily to them.

"I heard you were leaving us for a concert."

Wayne Newman's eyes darkened.

"Cops held me back. The sponsors are suing me."

"Surely it's not your fault?"

"Tell them that. You know how much money I lost?"

Jenny tried to bring the conversation back on track.

"How can I help you, Wayne?"

"Solve this whole mess as soon as possible. I can't afford to lose any more gigs."

"Didn't you get a role on TV?"

"Sure did," Wayne gloated. "But I'm a musician at heart. I'll stop breathing if I don't make music."

"Has being a TV star helped you get on tour?"

"I suppose it has. Why?"

"Being a TV star is important to you then?"

"What kind of question is that? They are calling me the hottest reality TV star of the decade."

"Wow! That's big."

Wayne glanced around the room, bobbing his head. Jenny wondered if he was nodding at an imaginary audience.

"I'm glad you came here, Wayne. I need to ask you some questions."

"Hey! I got nothing to hide."

"Shall we begin then?"

Wayne sat up straighter and winked at

Jenny. She took it as a sign to carry on.

"What happened to your arm?"

"Faulty landing," he griped. "That girl hit me as she fell to her death. I'm lucky I got away with some bruises."

"But your jump was successful?"

"I wouldn't say that!"

"Whose idea was it? This whole skydiving thing?"

"I wanted to make a big splash. A big statement, you know. I agreed to having a small wedding in the boondocks – no offense…"

"None taken."

"I thought arriving for my wedding in a

parachute would be spectacular enough for my fans. I have to keep them happy."

"I thought it was a secret wedding."

"Something always leaks to the press. I am sure there must have been some paparazzi present there."

Jenny figured he had given an anonymous tip to some reporters. Clearly, Wayne Newman didn't want to lose this opportunity to make a splash in the tabloids.

"Crystal was fine with that?"

Wayne gave a sneaky smile.

"She had no choice. I didn't tell her until the last minute."

“I’m guessing you didn’t tell her at all.”

“I called her from the airport,” Wayne admitted. “She didn’t have a choice at that point.”

“Why didn’t you both do it? That would have been even more spectacular.”

“Crystal won’t go near a small plane. And sky diving is so not her thing. We argued about it.”

Jenny quirked one eyebrow, encouraging Wayne to go on.

“What if the show wants her to do it, huh? She can’t say no to them. She’ll be under contract. I told her this would be good practice. But she wouldn’t hear a word.”

"But I thought you didn't tell her until the last minute."

"We talked about it," Wayne pursed his lips. "She forbid me to do it. I went ahead and called her from the airport."

Crystal Mars was marrying a douche bag. Jenny admitted he was a very attractive douche bag. He was probably loaded too.

"Did you know Bella Darling?"

"Not really. I might have met her at some event or other."

"What did she have against you?"

"You'll have to ask her that."

He laughed out at his own humor and

stopped when he saw neither Jenny nor Heather were joining in.

"Did she have anything against Crystal?"

"Crystal's a sweet girl. She's got her head in the right place."

"What does that mean?"

"These young girls are pitted against each other by the media. There's a lot of competition. Everyone tries to be one up on the other."

"So you are saying Crystal and Bella were rivals."

Wayne shrugged. Jenny assumed that meant yes.

"Did you see her when you climbed up in that plane? What exactly did you do that day?"

"I've done this whole sky diving thing before," Wayne began. "So I know the drill. Once the pilot knew I was licensed for a solo dive, I was pretty much on my own."

"It must be a small plane. Was there room for anyone to hide?"

"I don't know. I was so excited I wasn't paying attention to anything else."

"So you didn't see Bella at all that day?"

"Not until she dashed into me and fell into that cake."

"It must have been a shock."

"Shock? It's surreal. Even the best reality show writers couldn't have scripted this scene."

"Bella was wearing a dress exactly like Crystal's. What's that all about?"

"I don't know. They got it on sale?"

"You know better than that, Wayne. Crystal's dress was couture. They don't make too many of those."

"I don't know much about women's fashion."

"It appears that Bella Darling wanted to cause some kind of disruption at your wedding. Any idea why she would do that?"

"Must have been a publicity stunt, or a

spoof of some kind."

"Crystal says she didn't know Bella either."

"Maybe it was supposed to be a big joke. Bella would arrive next to me, say ta-da or something and we would all laugh it off."

"Nobody is laughing right now, Wayne."

"Do you think the TV people arranged it?"

"Why would they do that?"

"They might have wanted to use the segment for the show, or for promos or something."

"Why haven't they come forward then?"

Wayne shrugged.

"Look, I have no idea why this broad was doing this crazy thing. All I know is it put a damper on my wedding. And now Crystal won't marry me."

"But Crystal said you're the one who's refusing to tie the knot."

"You have it wrong. Crystal says she won't go ahead with the wedding until they find out who killed Bella. That's why she hired you."

Jenny decided Crystal and Wayne were definitely not on the same page.

"Why do you say someone killed Bella?

She could have jumped on her own."

"I know her chute was messed with. I have my sources."

Had the police already released a statement about the circumstances surrounding Bella's death? Jenny reminded herself to check on that.

"What if I was the real target?" Wayne asked. "Maybe I was supposed to wear the damaged chute."

"Do you have any enemies?"

"Plenty!"

"I'm not talking about petty rivalry. Is there someone who might want to kill you?"

Wayne turned pale.

“I never gave it much thought.”

“Maybe you should, Wayne. And I suggest you talk to the cops about it. Give them a list. If you were the real target, you might need protection.”

“Crystal could have been the target too,” Wayne said. “When I booked the dive, I booked it for a couple.”

“But you said Crystal is scared of sky diving.”

“A man can hope, can’t he? I thought she would make an exception for our wedding day.”

“You have given me a lot to think about, Wayne. I am glad we had a chance to talk."

"I'm at your disposal, lady. Just do whatever it takes to sort out this mess. We start shooting the reality show next month. I want to take Crystal on our honeymoon before that. And we need to get married first for that to happen."

"I am going to try," Jenny promised. "Will you let me know if you think of something else? You know where to find me."

"Sure will!" Wayne drawled.

Jenny stood up to leave, then remembered something Jason had said.

"Have you hired a lawyer, Wayne?"

"Why do I need a lawyer?"

If Wayne hadn't hired Jason, who had? Jenny thought about it as she walked back to the café. Her stomach rumbled with hunger and she realized she had spent almost a couple of hours talking to Wayne Newman.

"We sold out of everything," Petunia told her as soon as she walked in. "I hope Heather gave you lunch."

"She didn't."

"I haven't eaten either," Petunia told her. "We'll have to fix something quickly."

"I can make some omelets."

Jenny pulled leftovers from the refrigerator. She chopped down grilled veggies and chicken and shredded a leftover block of cheese. Golden omelets were sizzling on the grill soon after.

"Do you have enough for me?" a voice called from the door.

Heather Morse came in and joined them.

"I thought he would never leave. I missed lunch too, Jenny. Please, please give me something to eat."

"There's enough for everyone," Jenny said with a smile.

"So what do you think of Wayne Newman?" Heather asked, chewing a big bite of her omelet.

"Country music icon turned TV star?"

"He's lying."

Chapter 8

"Crystal is hiring a bodyguard," Heather told the Magnolias the next morning.

It was yet another bright and sunny day in Pelican Cove. The women were enjoying their daily coffee break on the deck outside the café.

"She really thinks she is in danger?" Jenny asked.

"She's not sure. But it's good for her image. One of the tabloids is doing a story on it."

Betty Sue stopped knitting for a moment and scowled at Heather.

"You've wasted enough time on those Hollywood people, Heather. All your chores are piling up."

"Like what, Grandma?" Heather asked.

Her brow had set in a frown. Jenny had never seen her argue with Betty Sue.

"Tourist season's here. We need to clean the whole house, do our usual spruce up, check on the towels and sheets…you know the list!"

"I'm taking care of all that."

"When?" Betty Sue demanded.

"Heather's always done her job, Betty

Sue," Petunia said, trying to calm them down. "What do you think of that box Mandy has put up?"

"What box?" Jenny asked.

"There's a big suggestion box at the town office. Mandy wants people to come up with ideas about how we can beautify Main Street. She's going to discuss them at the town hall meeting tonight."

"She could've come to me," Betty Sue frowned.

Betty Sue Morse was a force to reckon with in Pelican Cove. She was used to people coming to her for advice. When it came to town matters, she called the shots. Mayors came and went, but everyone knew Betty Sue was the real power center.

"Your mind is full of ideas for the town. Right, Betty Sue?" Star asked mischievously.

Betty Sue took the bait.

"Being a Morse used to mean something. What does this girl know, eh? She hasn't even been here a week."

"The Welcome sign has been broken for ten years," Petunia said. "I'm going to suggest they make a new one."

"Do you have concerts on the beach?" Jenny asked. "We used to have concerts by the river where I lived. It's a great way to draw people out."

"We have the summer festival," Star

told Jenny, "and we have a barbecue or two. The local band always strikes up a tune at these times."

"I'm talking about doing something on a larger scale," Jenny explained. "With a proper stage and professional bands. There can be a different band every weekend. We can advertise about it in advance so that people can plan ahead."

"Why don't you put that idea in the box?" Petunia asked eagerly.

"You can hire that Crystal's husband," Betty Sue quipped. "He's loitering here anyway. Maybe he will come to the show in a parachute."

Jenny thought of Bella Darling as soon as Betty Sue mentioned the parachute.

Her eyes hardened and she frowned.

"You're thinking of Bella, aren't you?" Heather asked. "Have you made any progress?"

"I'm going to talk to Adam again."

The older women exchanged meaningful glances as soon as Jenny mentioned Adam.

"Have you gone out with him yet?" Molly asked.

"He said something about grabbing dinner at Ethan's shack."

"Ethan's place is like the café," Petunia snorted. "That's not a date."

"If he's not ready…" Star said softly.

"The time isn't right, girls."

"Don't you ladies have anything better to do than planning my dates?" Jenny grumbled. "I'm going in to start lunch."

The group broke up after that.

Jenny wrote down her idea about concerts on the beach on a piece of paper. She thought of special discounts the local shops could offer for the concerts. It could be a big boost to business.

She whipped butter and sugar for frosting, thinking about Adam. She wanted to know what Wayne had shared with him.

"Why don't you eat something?" Petunia asked a few hours later.

The lunch crowd had dwindled and they finally had some time to themselves. Jenny placed two plates loaded with sandwiches and chips on the small table and poured sweet tea for the both of them.

"I'm going to drop these off for Mandy," she said shyly. "I know I'm not really a resident but I want us to win that contest."

"What are you saying, dear? You are one of us now."

Jenny walked over to the town office and asked someone for the suggestion box. Mandy waved at her from a conference room.

"Got some ideas for me?" she asked cheerfully.

Jenny explained her concept.

"I like that. I really like that. But I'm not sure it falls under beautification. It's more like cultural enrichment."

"Isn't that a kind of beauty too?" Jenny asked uncertainly.

"I'm not rejecting your suggestion, Jenny. We can discuss it during the meeting."

"I was thinking a bit higher than fresh paint."

"Fresh paint is important," Mandy said. "Have you looked at the places on Main Street? Really looked? Most of the places are crumbling. They haven't seen a coat of paint in years."

Jenny opened her mouth to object.

"Your café is one of them," Mandy went on. "It's an eyesore."

"The Boardwalk Café is the most popular spot on Main Street. Locals and tourists both flock to the place. We are already rushed off our feet and it's not even Memorial Day."

"That's because they don't have a choice," Mandy said glibly. "If a spanking new place opened next door, no one would step into that derelict café."

"Now you're insulting us."

"I'm just saying it like it is. It's my job."

"Being rude to people and attacking

their livelihood is what you do for a living?"

"Come on, Jenny! That's not what I meant. Offering suggestions for improvement is why the town hired me."

"You won't find many takers for your suggestions with that attitude," Jenny fumed.

She stormed out and walked to the police station. Adam Hopkins was next on her list.

"How are you, Jenny?" Adam asked her with a smile.

Jenny was taken aback. In the few months she had visited him at work, Adam Hopkins had rarely greeted her pleasantly.

"I guess you are here to volunteer some information about the crime."

"Are you feeling alright?" Jenny asked. "You don't sound like Adam at all."

"Ha ha!"

"I did want to share something with you."

"Fire away."

"Wayne Newman came to talk to me yesterday. Have you questioned him yet?"

"We talked to him once," Adam admitted. "Twice actually. The first was on the day of the wedding, or murder."

"Wayne thinks the tampered parachute may have been meant for him or Crystal. The earlier plan was for both of them to dive off that plane. Crystal refused because she is afraid of heights or something."

"We thought of that. I have asked both of them to give us a list of anyone they suspect. But I don't think anything will come of it."

"But why?"

"You develop a gut feel about these things. I am convinced Bella was the intended target."

"She's not even famous. Both Crystal and Wayne are more popular than Bella. They must have more enemies."

"We will follow all leads. I'm going to check the list they give me, Jenny."

"Anything new about Bella?"

"Nothing I can tell you."

Jenny hesitated. She wanted to stay and talk to Adam some more.

"That Mandy James is something else. She says the café is an eyesore."

"How dare she!"

"You can laugh all you want. I am worried she's out to get me."

"Don't be paranoid, Jenny. She barely knows you."

Jenny shot herself in the foot before she could stop herself.

"What about grabbing dinner at Ethan's tonight? I fancy some fried fish."

"Sorry, can't."

Jenny wished a sinkhole would appear next to her so she could disappear forever.

"I was just kidding," she giggled nervously.

Adam leaned forward and took her hand in his. His eyes softened as he looked at her.

"Jenny, I would love to go to Ethan's with you. But I can't tonight. I have to work."

"Okay."

"There's a town hall meeting tonight. Aren't you going with Star?"

"I'm not sure I am allowed to go."

"Why would anyone stop you? Almost everyone in town turns up for the meetings. They can be quite entertaining."

"Somehow I can't picture you enjoying a meeting of that kind."

"I don't! But I'm working tonight. They have a couple of cops on duty at these meetings. It's my turn."

"I see."

Jenny made some more small talk with Adam. She asked about his leg, asked about his twin daughters and talked about the weather. Finally, she could think of nothing else.

Adam looked at his watch and sighed.

"I hate to break this up, but I'm expecting someone."

"It's high time I left. I have to go to the seafood market before I go home."

Jenny almost collided with someone on her way out.

"Jenny!" a pair of arms grabbed her.

"Hey Jason!" she smiled back.

"I'm glad I ran into you. Are you going to the town hall meeting? Why don't we go together?"

"Do you want to have dinner with us?

I'm going to the market to get some fish."

"That sounds lovely! I'll see you then."

Jenny wondered what Jason was doing there.

"Got a meeting with Adam," he told her himself.

A young man stood next to Jason, scratching his head with a pen. Jenny rightly guessed he was a new client.

Dinner was light hearted with Jason regaling them with gossip from the city courts. They decided to walk to town.

"Who's your new client?" Jenny asked.

"You'll find out soon enough."

Jason bought some ice cream for them from the Pelican Cove Creamery. He handed over the plastic cups loaded with three large scoops of ice cream.

"Raspberry and chocolate!" Jenny exclaimed. "Yum!"

"Wait till you try their peach."

The room where the meeting was being held was packed when they went in. Petunia had saved seats for them. Heather and Molly sat next to her. Jenny spied Betty Sue sitting on a small raised platform, next to Barb Norton and a few other people. One of them was Ada Newbury, the richest woman in town. There was an old man Jenny recognized as Heather's grandpa. He and Betty Sue had been separated for several years.

"They are life members," Heather whispered to Jenny. "Barb may be the chairman of this particular committee but she can't totally ignore the rest of them. According to the guidelines, they have a vote anyway."

"And your grandma has veto power?"

"She kind of does," Heather said seriously, "although she hasn't exercised it in decades."

"Let's hope she doesn't have to make an exception this time."

Jenny told Heather and Petunia about her run in with Mandy James.

"How dare she!" Heather fumed. "She'll be attacking our inn next."

"I wouldn't put it past her," Jenny nodded.

According to her, Heather's inn was more vintage than the café.

An old man seated in the first row started grumbling about the time.

"That's Asher Cohen," Heather told Jenny. "He's a hundred years old."

Mandy James opened the suggestion box with great pomp and began reading the chits of paper one by one. People argued about every idea like their life depended on it. Jenny had never been to a meeting of this kind.

"Repaint the light house," Mandy read the next one. "The light house is not on Main Street, is it? Why are we even talking about it?"

A man in the front row struggled to his feet. He swayed on his feet, trying to maintain balance. Jenny guessed he had imbibed a bit too much as usual.

"Jimmy's here too?" Molly asked.

Jimmy Parsons was the town drunk. He lived in a small cottage next to the light house. Funnily enough, he owned the light house and the land it sat on.

"The light house is a Pelican Cove landmark, missy. It's what makes the town pretty."

Almost everyone present agreed to that. Mandy wasn't ready to consider it though.

the new reality show Crystal was a star in. Was it worth giving it all up for the sake of doing the right thing?

Raised in a devout Catholic family, Rainbow had flouted many tenets of her faith since she reached Hollywood. She had lied and cheated to get ahead. She had coveted what someone else had and she had frequently refused help to those in need. But she had never actually harmed anyone.

Bella Darling's face swam before her eyes. The poor girl had barely known life. She was like a younger sister to Rainbow. At least she had been until Rainbow jumped ship and joined the Crystal Mars camp. She had braved Crystal's ire and met Bella once. Tried hard to talk some sense into her.

Blinded by love, Bella had turned her back on Rainbow.

A couple of restless hours later, Rainbow came to a decision.

Jenny slammed a plate of soup on the counter and got some change from the cash register. She avoided looking up at the café's latest customer.

"Don't take it personally, Jenny. I'm just doing my job."

Jenny placed her hands on her hips and glared at Mandy James.

"This café has been around longer than you have, missy. Think twice before you make plans to tear it down."

"Who's talking about tearing it down?

You have it all wrong."

"I was there at the town hall meeting last night. I know what you said."

"All I meant is you need to fix up this place."

"Look around you. We are bursting at the seams. Most locals eat here twice a day. Tourists visiting town come and eat at our café year after year. Surely that means something."

"The town wants to win this contest. That's why they hired me. This particular contest calls for a pretty town. Face it, your café isn't pretty."

"Enjoy your lunch," Jenny spat and went into the kitchen.

Jenny had been smoldering since the town hall meeting. Mandy James and her vendetta against the Boardwalk Café had been the main topic of discussion among the Magnolias that morning. They had banded together and vowed to do anything they could to protect their café.

"I'm glad you're standing up for me, Jenny," Petunia said emotionally.

"I don't understand why she is picking on us."

"That Mandy James has come up with a long list. We are not the only ones on her radar."

"She's being too literal, don't you think? I love the idea of repainting the light house. It will give the whole town a face lift."

"She's got a bunch of ideas for Main Street. Fresh flower beds at every corner, murals on building walls, Victorian lamp posts…she wants to color code the trash cans and benches and provide free bicycles for everyone."

"Bicycles?"

"She wants to keep the cars off Main Street. People can either walk or borrow one of these bikes."

Jenny rolled her eyes, making her disdain clear.

There was a knock on the kitchen door and a blonde face peeped in.

"Can I come in?"

"You are from Crystal's wedding party, aren't you?" Petunia asked the girl.

"I'm Rainbow," she said, looking at Jenny. "We met the other day."

"Of course! Come on in. Do you want a table on the deck out back?"

"I'm here by myself," Rainbow said hesitantly. "Can I talk to you?"

"Have you had lunch, dear?" Petunia asked, ladling thick tomato soup into a bowl. "Jenny and I were just sitting down to eat."

Rainbow admitted she had missed lunch.

"Can we eat first?" Jenny asked.

Rainbow nodded and began slurping the tomato soup. Petunia served them hot grilled cheese sandwiches off the grill.

"I never get to eat carbs," Rainbow exclaimed. "Crystal would kill me for this."

"How does it matter to her?" Jenny asked. "You can eat anything if you are blessed with a good metabolism."

"Which I am, thankfully," the girl said, bringing her palms together and closing her eyes for a second. "It's all about image. Appearances mean a lot in Hollywood."

"I've heard. But where does Crystal come in?"

"Crystal has allowed me in her inner circle. I have to toe the line if I want to stay there."

"You mean you're part of some elite posse which Crystal rules over?"

"The entire wedding party is," the girl explained. "Other than you and Heather, we are all 'her girls'. We dress a certain way, and eat according to a diet plan her nutritionist comes up with. Her stylist tells us what to wear."

"That's great. So you get free fashion advice from a pro."

"It's not fashion advice exactly. We can only wear certain colors, or certain styles on a given day. It's all coordinated to make Crystal stand out."

"She's a star. Isn't she supposed to be a notch above the rest anyway?"

"That takes work," Rainbow said.

She clammed up after that, realizing she had spoken too much.

"You are so beautiful," Jenny praised. "I'm sure you have great things in store for you."

Rainbow blushed like the young girl she was. She looked longingly at the cupcakes Jenny offered her but refused to taste them.

"What brings you here, Rainbow?"

"You were going to find out what happened to Bella."

“That’s right.”

“What if it’s someone connected to Crystal?”

Jenny’s face clouded as she looked at Rainbow.

“Is there something I should know?”

“I’m not sure how much you have found out.”

“I’m just starting out, Rainbow. If you know something about Bella, I suggest you come clean. You can talk to the cops directly. Or I can go with you.”

“No cops,” Rainbow said immediately. “I need to keep this quiet.”

“Why don’t you tell me what it is first?”

"Wayne was having an affair with Bella," Rainbow blurted out.

"What? But he said he didn't know her."

"He knew her very well. A bit too well."

"How long have you known about this?"

"Three months or so."

"Does Crystal know this?"

"I don't know."

"Does anyone else know?"

"I'm not sure, Jenny."

"Was this after Crystal and Wayne were

engaged?"

"Oh yes."

"How did you find out? Did you come upon them somewhere?"

"Bella used to be my roommate. I moved out when Crystal picked me but I continued to meet Bella."

"She told you about Wayne?"

"Wayne has a reputation with the ladies. I warned her about him but she ignored me."

"Did she know about Wayne and Crystal? I understand their engagement has been hush-hush."

"She did later. But she refused to stop

seeing Wayne."

"What was she doing up there on that plane?"

"I've been trying to figure that out. Maybe she wanted to talk Wayne out of it."

"Do you know her parachute had been slashed? Who would do that to her?"

Rainbow suddenly looked frightened.

"I just wanted to tell you about Bella and Wayne. Can you promise you'll keep this between us?"

"You need to tell the police about this. According to Wayne's statement, he did not know Bella at all."

"That's a lie!"

"Do you have any proof about this?"

"We went out to dinner once," Rainbow remembered. "We took some selfies but Wayne made us delete them."

"He knows you knew about him and Bella?"

Rainbow nodded fearfully.

"We never talk about it, especially around Crystal."

"Does Wayne love Crystal? Why are they getting married?"

"Wayne Newman will do anything to further his career. So will Crystal. They are made for each other."

"So neither of them actually loves the other?"

"I've said too much," Rainbow said, picking up her bag. "I just wanted to tell you about Bella."

"Thanks for coming here," Jenny nodded, giving her a hug. "And don't worry. I won't go telling tales to Crystal."

Petunia had been cleaning up outside while Rainbow talked with Jenny. She came in after Rainbow left.

"What did she want with you?"

"Nothing much," Jenny said diplomatically.

She began slicing strawberries for the shortcake she planned to make the next morning. A couple of hours later, she walked to the police station.

Adam Hopkins was out and she decided to head on home. It had been a busy day at the café and her feet were killing her.

Jenny and Star ate dinner in front of the TV, watching Gilmore Girls reruns.

"Skipping your walk today?" Star asked her after the sun went down.

"I would love to but I don't have that luxury. My pants are getting tighter by the day."

Star gave her a knowing smile.

"Honey, we both know what your motivation is behind these evening walks."

Jenny took the high road and said nothing.

Jenny laced up her sneakers and stepped out of her aunt's house. She gazed up at the neighboring house and crossed her fingers. Bending down to sniff at a climbing rose, she inhaled deeply and closed her eyes for a moment. Could it all really be hers?

Jenny had never imagined she would be so happy in Pelican Cove.

A bark sounded in the distance and Tank came running up to her. Jenny laughed as he placed his paws on her shoulders, his tail wagging furiously.

"How are you, handsome?"

"Are you talking to me?" a deep voice she had been yearning for all day spoke.

"Of course not!"

Adam grinned and surprised her by taking her arm in his.

"How are you, Jenny? Done any sleuthing today?"

"I do have something to tell you."

Adam looked astonished when Jenny finished talking.

"I'm not surprised Wayne Newman lied to us. I had him pegged as a fraud."

"It's hard to say who the villain is here. Could she have been blackmailing him?"

"That's possible. But we won't know that now."

"At least not until Wayne tells us that."

"The girl was barely 22, Jenny. She doesn't seem like she would hold out for money."

"Maybe she wanted something more. She could have real feelings for Wayne."

"Is that your woman's intuition, Jenny?"

Jenny pursed her lips, her uncertainty clear on her face.

"You never know with these

Hollywood types. They will do anything to get ahead in their careers."

"What could Wayne Newman offer her?"

"Name? Fame? A role in his latest TV series?"

"That's the same one Crystal Mars is in?"

Jenny shrugged.

"I can understand why Wayne didn't tell us about Bella. He's about to get married and she's gone anyway. Why dredge up the past?"

"What if the past had everything to do with Bella's murder?"

"So Bella tried to blackmail Wayne and he silenced her?"

Adam was quiet.

"It's not farfetched," Jenny admitted. "People have lost their lives for less."

"There's something you don't know yet. It could change the whole equation."

Chapter 10

"Mandy James has commissioned someone from Virginia Beach to paint the welcome sign," Molly told the Magnolias one morning.

"What a disgrace!" Betty Sue roared. "Why do we need an out-of-towner when we have our own resident artist?"

Star tried to calm them down.

"She must have a reason. I have never painted a welcome sign."

"You know how to paint, don't you?" Jenny asked her aunt. "Are you saying you can't paint 'Welcome to Pelican Cove' on a piece of wood?"

"What about the murals?" Heather demanded. "Has she commissioned you for them yet, Star?"

Star shook her head.

"She is going to have the school kids do that."

"Nonsense!" Betty Sue fumed. "We want art, not graffiti."

"This guy she hired in Virginia Beach is an award winning artist," Petunia informed them. "He's done welcome signs for many towns and these towns then went on to win some kind of award."

"Oh please!" Jenny snorted.

"Think of the devil…" Heather muttered and tipped her head toward the boardwalk.

Barb Norton was walking purposefully toward the café. Mandy James tagged along. The ladies climbed up the stairs to the deck and sat down.

Mandy James handed over an envelope to Petunia.

"What's this?"

"Just some work you need to get done in the next few weeks."

Petunia tore open the envelope and pulled out a sheet of paper.

"New shingles? I just replaced them five years ago."

"Every building on Main Street needs new shingles. You don't want to be the odd one out, do you?"

"Has everyone else agreed?" Jenny asked.

"They don't have much choice," Barb spoke up. "This is a town decree."

"What if we refuse?" Petunia asked.

"You will have to pay a hefty fine. Trust me, you don't want to go that route."

"Who signed off on that?" Betty Sue asked, holding her hand out for the paper.

Barb gave some lengthy explanation.

"That means nothing. I may have to use my veto power."

"Don't you want Pelican Cove to win the competition?" Mandy James asked.

"Of course we do," Petunia wailed. "But at what cost?"

"I know the people who judge these contests," Mandy said. "I know what they are looking for. You're not even close. Pelican Cove needs a complete makeover."

"So you want us to lose our identity?" Heather scowled. "What good is a prize if we have to mutate into something else to win it?"

"We are just going to gussy up the town, Heather," Barb Norton spoke. "Surely no one can object to that."

"Are you done yet?" Betty Sue railed. "I think you should leave now."

Barb Norton stood up with a huff and dragged Mandy to her feet. She stomped down the stairs to the beach but turned back for a parting shot.

"I am the chair of this committee, Betty Sue Morse. I am going to do whatever it takes to win this contest."

"What's going on here?" Star moaned, rubbing her temples. "Barb's like a dog with a bone. Just give her what she wants."

Petunia handed over the paper she had

been reading from.

“This is ridiculous!” Star agreed after she read a few items on the list. “It’s going to cost a fortune.”

“And I don’t have that kind of money,” Petunia said, looking worried.

“We’ll take a look at it later today,” Jenny consoled her. “We can prioritize some things. We’ll all pitch in, Petunia.”

The group broke up after that and Jenny went out to the cash register. A man sitting at a window table got up when he saw her.

“Are you Jenny King?” he asked timidly. “I have been looking for you.”

The man seemed vaguely familiar to

Jenny. He was just a few inches taller than her own five feet four inches and very ordinary in appearance.

“Have we met before?”

“I don’t think so.” He raised his eyebrows questioningly. “Can we talk somewhere?”

Jenny ushered him out to the deck and sat down at a small table.

“How do you know me?” she began.

“My lawyer told me about you.”

Jenny immediately connected the dots.

“You were with Jason that day…”

“That’s right. I’m Ray Fox. Bella’s husband.”

"Husband?" Jenny asked incredulously. "Bella Darling was married?"

"She sure was. We were coming up on our one year anniversary."

"Why didn't anyone mention it?"

"Nobody knew," Ray Fox said. "Bella wanted it that way."

Jenny could think of a few reasons why.

Ray hastened to explain.

"Hollywood has certain expectations. They want their girls young and single. A struggling actress loses value as soon as she ties the knot."

Jenny wasn't sure she believed that. She tried to keep the sarcasm out of her voice.

"Lots of Hollywood stars are married. Some even have kids."

"I guess you can call the shots when you become a star."

His face fell suddenly and he looked away. Bella Darling was never going to be a star now.

"What am I thinking?" Jenny exclaimed. "I'm sorry for your loss, Mr. Fox. I didn't know your wife but I am sure she was a good person."

"Please call me Ray," he said softly. "Bella was the best. She was so young."

"Was she really just twenty two?"

"She was, unlike some of the gals who just pretend to be so."

"How can I help you, Ray?"

"Jason told me you are working for Crystal Mars?"

"Crystal has asked me to look into what happened," Jenny agreed. "I am going to do just that. I will report whatever I find to the police. The truth will come out, Ray, whatever it is."

"Even if Crystal Mars is to blame?"

Jenny nodded.

"Jason told me you couldn't be bought."

"I'm not a professional detective, Ray.

I'm just a middle aged divorced woman who is talking to people and asking a few questions. I can't guarantee what I will find."

"I am thankful for your efforts, Jenny," Ray Fox said.

His eyes filled up as he spoke.

"Why would anyone want to kill my sweet Bella?"

Jenny patted Ray on the shoulder and tried to console him.

"Can you tell me something about her?"

"She was the best of friends," he began. "We were friends first, lovers later."

"How did you two meet?"

"Sky diving," Ray said with a smile. "We were both mad about it."

"So Bella had been sky diving before?"

"She had hundreds of solo jumps under her belt. She went up almost every weekend."

"And you met her at one of these places?"

"We both got our certifications around the same time. I'm a producer for a sitcom. We connected instantly, being from the industry."

"Does she have any family?"

"She dropped out of school and ran

away from home when she was a teen. Her family wrote her off, I guess. She planned to go back home when she made it big."

"Surely they tried to contact her?"

"They might have. But Bella never talked about it. I saw her looking at some photos once on Facebook. She shut it down when I asked her about it."

"I don't care that they had a falling out. I would want to know if anything happened to my kid."

"I agree," Ray Fox said. "But Darling was a stage name. I am not sure what her real name was. She was Bella Darling when I met her. She got her driver's license changed too."

“Why did you decide to get married?”

“I fell for her hook, line and sinker. Bella didn’t want to get tied down though. She signed a contract that forbid her from marrying while the show ran. Something went wrong and they dropped her at the last minute.”

“Did it have anything to do with Crystal?”

“I can’t confirm that. But Crystal did replace her.”

“Did they know each other personally?”

“I doubt it.”

“What happened then?”

“Bella went into a funk after that. She was barely making ends meet. I proposed again, told her it could be temporary until she got back on her feet.”

“So she agreed to marry you.”

“I would like to think she was in love with me at least a little. But maybe she just got tired of starving.”

“Don’t be too hard on yourself, Ray,” Jenny soothed.

“We weren’t destined to be together after all.”

“Did Bella have any enemies?”

“Bella was friends with everyone. She could be too nice sometimes. That’s not how you get ahead in the entertainment industry."

"You can't think of anyone who might have wanted to harm her?"

Ray shook his head.

"You know this new reality show Crystal is doing? Bella got the short end of the stick. She's the one who should have had a grudge against Crystal."

"Is that why she wanted to ruin Crystal's wedding?"

"I have no idea. I was shooting on location with my unit. I didn't even know Bella had come to Virginia."

"Did they tell you about the wedding dress she was wearing?"

"Vera Wang was her favorite designer."

"Where did she get hold of that dress?"

"She knew a lot of people who worked in the fashion industry. She must have traded in a favor."

"Crystal Mars was wearing the exact same dress."

"She was? Bella must have been wearing a copy then."

"What about the sapphire around her neck?"

"I have never seen it before. It must have cost a fortune."

"Do you think she stole it?"

Ray looked indignant.

“Bella wouldn’t do that. She must have borrowed it from someone.”

“Did she know people who owned that kind of jewelry?”

“She was friendly with a lot of famous people. She had a few irons in the fire. She would have landed a big role pretty soon. I don’t think she really cared about Crystal Mars one way or the other.”

“What would have happened if Bella had landed successfully at the wedding? Was it some kind of publicity stunt?”

“Bella wasn’t like that. I really don’t understand why she was there.”

Jenny thought over her next words before she spoke.

"Bella was having an affair with Wayne Newman."

Ray Fox exploded.

"That's a load of crap! Bella would never cheat on me."

Jenny said nothing.

Ray Fox got up and paced on the deck, muttering to himself. Jenny let him fume. He came and sat down after a while.

"Are you sure about this?" he begged.

"Only two people can confirm this. Bella's gone. Wayne Newman said he didn't know her."

"That's a lie," Ray burst out. "Wayne

knew Bella."

"Did they date each other?"

"Bella went out with him a couple of times. This was before we got married."

"So you knew about it and you still married her?"

"It wasn't like that. Wayne was trying to woo her. This was back when she was supposed to star in that TV series. When the network dropped her, Wayne followed suit. She was glad. She said he was a jerk."

"So why did she cheat on you, Ray?"

"There's only one reason Bella would have done it," Ray said. "He must have offered her something I can't."

"Didn't you say she hated him?"

Ray shrugged. He leaned forward and stared into Jenny's eyes.

"You don't have to look any further. Wayne Newman killed my wife."

"That's quite an allegation, Ray."

"It's the truth though."

"Where were you on the day of Crystal's wedding?"

"Back home in L.A."

"Can someone vouch for that?"

"I was home alone, wondering where my wife was," Ray said grimly. "I had no idea my wife was thousands of miles away, jumping to her death."

Chapter 11

Jenny and Heather were driving to the Pelican Cove Country Club again. Jenny wanted to talk to Crystal. A lot of new facts had come to light since she last spoke to her. Spooked by the alleged threat against her life, Crystal had gone to ground at the club.

A maid led them to a verandah overlooking the golf course. Crystal sat at a table, drinking iced tea. A tall, hefty man stood at attention a few feet away. Jenny rightly guessed he was the bodyguard Crystal had hired.

"How are you holding up, Crystal?"

Crystal gave an exaggerated sigh.

"Why do these things happen to me? This was supposed to be my honeymoon. Here I am, watching over my shoulder, running for my life."

"Be thankful you have a life," Heather told her.

Crystal motioned toward the man standing nearby.

"I'm taking this very seriously. Wayne told me what happened to Bella's parachute. I am convinced someone wanted to kill me."

"Why would they do that?" Jenny asked. "Do you have a lot of enemies?"

"People are jealous," Crystal pouted. "A star's life is not easy. You're under the radar all the time and people are waiting for you to slip up."

"I can understand that," Jenny agreed. "There's a lot of competition. That doesn't mean people go around killing each other."

"The parachute is proof, isn't it?"

"How many people knew you were going to jump from the plane, Crystal?"

"I would never have done that. I'm afraid of heights."

"What if someone paid you a big amount of money to do it?"

"They wanted me to do it for the show.

I refused. I got my lawyer to add a clause. Sky diving, bungee jumping, zip lining – none of that crazy stuff."

Jenny wondered why the network had hired Crystal.

"So someone who knows you well would know you would never go up in that plane."

Crystal nodded emphatically.

"The whole unit knew it, right from the producers to the camera guys."

Jenny lapsed into thought. If anyone had wanted to hurt Crystal, they would have chosen a different method.

"Have you remembered anything about Bella?"

“I told you, Jenny. I didn’t know the girl.”

“She was having an affair with Wayne Newman.”

“I’m not naïve. I know Wayne’s been around the block. We both have. So what?”

“You were okay with him cheating on you?”

“Who said anything about cheating?”

“He was engaged to you, wasn’t he?”

“Wait a minute. Are you suggesting he was seeing Bella after we were engaged?”

Jenny nodded.

"Who told you that?"

"Never mind who told me. Did you know anything about it?"

Crystal's eyes hardened.

"I didn't."

"Would you have broken off the engagement if you knew?"

"Probably not."

Jenny was taken aback. She was surprised Crystal was being so upfront. But she didn't understand why Crystal was so desperate to get married."

Crystal leaned forward and whispered in Jenny's ear.

"I turned thirty this year."

Jenny reacted appropriately.

"I thought you were in your early twenties."

Crystal gloated a bit.

"I work very hard to look that way, Jenny. What I mean is, I have an expiry date. Turning thirty is like a death sentence in the industry. I can pull it off for some time, maybe. But the roles will start drying up in a couple of years. I need to make my fortune before that."

"Sounds harsh."

"That's just the way it is."

"What does this have to do with Wayne cheating on you?"

"Wayne's very popular right now. Being his wife will elevate my status instantly. I need that, Jenny."

"So you are willing to overlook a few transgressions like an affair or two."

"Neither of us are kids. Our rose colored glasses have been ripped off long ago."

"Why is Wayne marrying you? Does he love you even a little bit?"

"He says he does," Crystal laughed shrilly. "We both have something to offer each other."

"How far will you go? We already know Wayne's a womanizer. What if he does drugs? What if he is abusive?"

"I can deal with all that once we are married. It will make great news copy. The tragic wife! I can earn a lot of sympathy from the fans."

Jenny stole a glance at Heather. Heather's shock was evident in her expression.

"You mean you're marrying Wayne even after knowing all this bad stuff?"

"Heather, you're such a sweetie. I'm marrying him because I know these things."

Jenny wondered what kind of twisted world Crystal Mars lived in.

"Where do you draw the line?" she exploded. "What if Wayne wanted you out of the way?"

"He wouldn't do that! We have an understanding."

"What if he got rid of Bella?"

"He could have dumped her any time. No one gave a damn about Bella Darling."

Jenny slapped her hand on the table.

"Are you being stupid on purpose? What if Wayne tampered with that parachute, Crystal? Would you still want to marry him?"

"Wayne had no reason to do that. Don't you have any other suspects?"

"Wayne's the only one who had an opportunity to harm Bella. He was up there with her on that plane."

“Why would he do it on our wedding day?”

“I don’t have an answer for that. Have you come up with any other names?”

“Maybe someone wanted to hold up my wedding.”

“That’s a stretch.”

“Bella might have gotten away with a broken arm or leg. Why did she have to die?”

“It’s hard to predict what will happen when a person drops from ten thousand feet. Only a fool could have thought that.”

“Have you met the girls? They are not really bright, Jenny.”

"Are you saying one of your bridesmaids did it?"

Crystal shrugged.

"They could have."

"Do you really believe that?"

Crystal settled back in her chair and looked around. She stifled a yawn and looked at Jenny.

"This is all a big waste of time. I am sure this was an accident. Bella was just unlucky."

"Didn't we just talk about the slashed parachute?" Jenny asked her. "Pay attention, Crystal. This was no accident. Someone very definitely wanted Bella out of the way. This is a murder investigation."

"The police said that. I thought they were bluffing to get some reaction out of me."

Jenny wanted to tell Crystal the police didn't bluff about such things.

"Did any of your bridesmaids know Bella?" Heather asked.

She didn't know about Jenny's talk with the girl called Rainbow.

"Rainbow did."

"Were they friends?" Heather went on.

"Anything but," Crystal snorted.

"What was that?" Jenny asked sharply.

"Rainbow hated Bella. They got into a big fight. She got Bella banned from the set."

"But I thought Bella wasn't part of your show?"

"This was before they signed me on. There was some scandal and Bella got fired."

Jenny's head was spinning with possibilities.

Crystal clutched the bridge of her nose suddenly. She closed her eyes and started massaging her temples.

"Are we done here? I think I'm getting a migraine."

Jenny and Heather expressed their

sympathy. They took a circuitous route back to the car.

"She could've offered us a drink," Heather complained. "I'm dying from thirst."

"I'll make you a smoothie when we get back to the café," Jenny promised.

She was deep in thought. She couldn't figure out who was lying, Rainbow or Crystal? Rainbow had claimed to be friends with Bella.

"Did you feel we were going around in circles?" Heather asked.

"Led by Crystal," Jenny nodded. "Is she always like this?"

"Like what?"

"A bit dumb."

"I don't know her that well, Jenny."

"She is either completely hare brained or very clever. Wanna bet it's the latter?"

"Did you believe all that stuff about marrying Wayne inspite of knowing bad things about him?"

"Exactly! How do we know she wasn't on to the affair? She could have wanted revenge on Bella."

"Why would she want to ruin her own wedding?"

"That's exactly why. No one would suspect her of doing it."

They spotted a bunch of girls seated in a gazebo overlooking the ocean. One of the girls waved at them and walked over.

"Hello," Rainbow said, smiling sweetly at Jenny. "Were you here to meet Crystal?"

Jenny nodded.

"Can you walk with us? I would like to ask you a few questions."

Rainbow fell in step with them. Jenny waited until they were a good distance away from the gazebo.

"You told me you were friends with Bella."

"Of course! We shared an apartment

for some time."

"According to Crystal, you didn't get along at all. She says you got Bella fired."

Rainbow froze, looking like a deer in the headlights. Jenny placed her hands on her hips and quirked an eyebrow questioningly.

"I may not have told you everything," Rainbow mumbled.

"You hated Bella, didn't you?"

"We had a falling out," Rainbow agreed. "But we weren't always like that. I treated her like a younger sister."

"What went wrong?"

"She stabbed me in the back," Rainbow said bitterly. "I didn't see it coming. She acted all innocent, you know. But it was all fake."

"What did she do?"

"I'd rather not talk about it."

"Were you angry with her?"

"She made me so mad!"

"Mad enough to kill?"

Rainbow gasped.

"What? Of course not. This kind of thing is very common. That doesn't mean we go around killing people."

"But someone did kill Bella. Or have you forgotten that?"

"Look, I thought about what you said. Maybe Crystal was the target here."

"Crystal said she's afraid of heights."

"She is. But she'll do anything for a bit of attention."

"Any update on the wedding?"

"Wayne is still holding out. Crystal's trying to convince him."

"How long are you going to stick around?"

Rainbow shrugged.

"We haven't been cleared to leave yet. We don't mind though. This place is so beautiful. It's like an impromptu vacation."

"You didn't tell me Bella was married."

Rainbow looked away, refusing to say anything.

"Why did Bella have an affair with Wayne? Did he promise her something?"

"I don't know. Bella wasn't sharing stuff with me by that time."

"Was Wayne forcing her, do you think?"

"Have you seen Wayne Newman?" Rainbow exhaled. "He doesn't force women. They fall at his feet, begging to be noticed."

Jenny wondered if there was a note of bitterness in Rainbow's voice.

"That dinner you had with Bella and Wayne? Did that really happen?"

"It did," Rainbow said.

"Let me know if you think of anything else, Rainbow."

Jenny and Heather waved goodbye and walked to their car. It was a considerable distance away.

"Shouldn't they offer us those golf cart things?" Heather complained.

Jenny pulled a tissue out of her bag and mopped her brow. The car had been toasting out in the sun. Jenny turned the air conditioner on full blast and stuck her face in front of the vents.

"I could use a cold shower right about

now," she groaned.

"I'm getting a headache," Heather said.

She pointed back toward the club.

"Crystal doesn't seem like a good person, does she?"

"She's single minded. I'll say that for her."

"Sometimes I feel I lead a very sheltered life," Heather confessed.

"There's a big bad world out there, kiddo. Pelican Cove is like our own bit of paradise."

"I'm glad you came here, Jenny. I know you're a bit older than me but I like having you for a friend."

"Anymore of that and you'll make Chris jealous," Jenny joked.

"Chris has forgotten I exist."

"Weren't you complaining he was getting too close?" Jenny teased.

"I guess I spoke too soon."

Chapter 12

Mandy James walked along Main Street, waving her phone in the air.

"What is she doing now?" Petunia asked Jenny.

"I think she's taking pictures."

"She couldn't use the ones we have in the town archives?"

The ladies at the Boardwalk Café were enjoying a respite after the breakfast rush. Mandy walked in a few minutes later with Barb Norton in tow.

"Can I have one of your famous chocolate cupcakes? The ones with the raspberry frosting?"

"Sure," Jenny drawled. "Can I get you anything else?"

Mandy took the cupcake out on the deck. She fiddled around with it, putting it on different spots on a table. She took pictures from different angles, climbing up on a chair once to take a top shot. She finally cried in triumph and sat down in one of the chairs.

"What are the photos for?" Jenny asked.

"Pelican Cove is now on Instagram. I'm taking pictures of the best things the town has to offer. The beaches, sand dunes, the flowering trees, anything that will make people flock to Pelican Cove."

"I thought your focus was on Main Street."

"It is. But Main Street is not up to snuff yet. I will start taking photos after the refurbishment."

"So you want to take before and after photos?"

"Not really. Some things don't need a makeover, like the ocean and your delicious cupcakes."

Jenny looked at Mandy suspiciously.

"What do you want, Mandy?"

Mandy dropped all pretense.

"You have Petunia's ear. Please get her to go through the list I sent. You guys need to start on those improvements right away."

"I'm not sure she can afford them."

"That's a problem, Jenny."

"Are you going to force us to shut down?"

"A defunct business will look worse. The café is just too prominent."

"What would you have us do?"

"Get a facelift. Get with the program. Don't you want your town to win? You win once but you can carry the tag forever."

"Is that your usual spiel?"

"You're from the city, aren't you? I thought we'd be on the same page. What can you do to make these hicks see the light? I'll make it worth your while."

Jenny bristled at the suggestion. Her hands went to her hips and she glared at Mandy James.

"Get out. Now."

"Don't get me wrong, Jenny. At least read the list. Please?"

"Alright. I'll give it a look."

Mandy James walked down the steps to the beach.

"What did she want, dear?" Petunia asked, coming out of the kitchen.

"Nothing in particular. Forget about it."

Heather arrived some time later with Betty Sue. Molly wasn't far behind. Petunia told them about Mandy.

"That Mandy James was walking around clicking pictures."

"Does Barb know that?" Betty Sue asked, pulling a ball of blue wool from her bag.

"Barb was following her around. Jenny knows all about it."

Jenny told them about the Instagram.

"What is that?" Betty Sue thundered.

"It's like Facebook, grandma, but it's different."

"How is that going to help us win?"

"Why don't we go over the list you have, Petunia? Maybe we should ask a contractor for an estimate."

"We may not need a contractor," Heather told them. "We can get the guys to pitch in, have a potluck. Everyone will help."

Jenny didn't look convinced.

"What if there's some structural work to be done?"

"The list is not going to tell you that,"

Petunia argued. "We will need to get an inspector here to check on everything."

"I say let's do that," Jenny urged. "Let's get an estimate for a complete makeover."

"Are you out of your mind?" Petunia asked. "I don't have that kind of money."

"What's the harm in getting an estimate?"

Jenny widened her eyes at Heather. She caught on immediately.

"Bring that list out. We can check off the easy things."

"That's it then. We know what we can do ourselves. We'll get an estimate for the rest."

"Can you imagine Mandy's face if we do all of this?" Heather squealed.

"Don't get ahead of yourself, girls. There's no way I can get all this done."

"Any update on that poor girl?" Betty Sue asked.

"I learn something new every day. She was married, for instance. She had an affair with Crystal's fiancé."

"Maybe she wasn't as innocent as she looks," Molly said.

"She is the victim here, Molls," Jenny reminded her.

She looked at the rest of them.

"Everyone I talk to is lying about something. I am not sure I can trust anyone."

"You should take some advice from Adam," Betty Sue hinted. "See what he thinks."

"Adam keeps things close to his chest," Jenny complained. "He's not going to help."

"So what's the plan?" Molly asked her.

"I'm not sure," Jenny admitted reluctantly. "I'm still thinking."

She took Betty Sue's advice to heart later that day and decided to go meet Adam. Adam was having a bad day.

"What is it, Jenny?" he scowled. "I'm

busy."

Jenny sat down and smiled at him. She had brought over a plate of cupcakes for the staff. She was sure no one would disturb them.

"How's the leg?"

"As usual…what do you want?"

"How are the twins? Are they coming home soon?"

Adam banged a fist on the desk.

"Jenny, I don't have time for small talk. What do you want?"

"Can't I just come in to say hello?"

"Of course you can," Adam sighed. "But I really don't have time to take a break."

"Are you working on Bella's case?"

Adam rolled his eyes and tried not to grin.

"So you're on a hunting expedition."

Jenny shrugged.

"I talked to Wayne and Crystal. And Bella's husband came to talk to me."

"Good for you. If it were up to me, none of them would have told you anything."

"Did you know Bella was having an affair with Wayne?"

Adam sat up with a start.

"What?"

"Bella and Wayne had an affair."

"Where do you learn these things?"

"I can be useful to you, Adam. We should work together."

"Be serious, Jenny. How sure are you about this?"

"They definitely had an affair before Bella got married. And they were still seeing each other."

"Even though that Wayne guy was engaged?"

Jenny nodded.

"That changes everything."

It was Jenny's turn to be surprised.

"You are hiding something from me."

"I am not," Adam argued. "That's because I am not required to tell you anything."

"We can agree on that. Now can you please tell me?"

Adam was quiet for a minute.

"Bella was pregnant."

Jenny let out a cry.

"Oh! That poor girl. How far along was she?"

Jenny tried to remember if Bella Darling had been showing her baby bump on that fateful day. She realized she hadn't really looked closely.

"A couple of months, according to the autopsy report."

"It could be Wayne's."

"You realize what this means, don't you?" Adam asked. "This is a double murder."

"You're right," Jenny said softly.

She sat stunned for a few minutes, saying nothing. Then she remembered something Ray Fox had said.

"What about the sapphire?"

"She was supposed to wear it for a photo shoot," Adam explained. "That's how she got her hands on such an expensive piece."

"Have you cleared Ray Fox?"

"He doesn't have an alibi so he's still under suspicion."

"What about the pilot of the plane?"

"What about him, Jenny?"

"I should go talk to him."

"You are meddling in an ongoing investigation again."

"I'm just trying to find out what happened, Adam. I want to help."

"You are neither trained nor qualified for this," Adam fumed. "Stop putting yourself in danger."

"Nothing's happening to me!" Jenny brushed Adam off.

"Are you done now?"

"Do you know our town is now on Instagram?"

"I don't want to know. I'll see you later, Jenny."

Jenny decided Adam was about to flip. She got up and said goodbye.

"Just one more thing…"

"Now what?"

"Can you recommend a good contractor?"

Adam scribbled something on a notepad and tore the paper off. He handed it to Jenny.

"Now don't bother me for a couple of weeks."

Jenny laughed on her way out. She saw Adam's face break into a smile through the corner of her eye. So he wasn't completely immune to her. She hoped he would hurry up and ask her out on a proper date.

Jenny walked to the seafood market. Chris Williams greeted her with a smile and a hug.

"Where have you been hiding, Chris? You haven't come to the café in a long time."

"We did our annual inventory," he explained. "Restocked everything.

Getting ready for tourist season, you know."

"I'm not the only one who's feeling neglected."

Chris blushed.

"Did Heather say something? I thought she was busy at the country club."

"Not really. She misses you, Chris."

'You want to go on a double date? We can take the boat out one evening. You, me, Heather and Jason…"

"Sounds great," Jenny nodded. "Now how about some trout?"

Jenny remembered she was out of Old Bay seasoning. It was an absolutely essential ingredient on the Eastern Shore. Star wouldn't eat fish unless it was liberally sprinkled with the signature spice.

She almost collided with someone in the spice aisle.

"Jenny!" Ray Fox stared back at her.

His eyes were bloodshot and his clothes looked like he had slept in them. Jenny wondered if he knew what Adam had told her.

"What are you doing here, Ray?"

"I don't know. Just walking around."

Jenny picked up a bottle of seasoning, trying to think of what to say next.

There was a haunted look in his eyes.

“We talked about giving it all up, Bella and I. We dreamed of moving to a small town by the sea, just like this one. Somewhere we could raise our kids, far away from the shadow of Hollywood.”

“Any luck with Bella’s family?”

Ray shook his head.

“I’m trying to reach out to some of her friends, girls she knew when she first moved to Los Angeles. They might know something.”

“Why don’t you come over to the café tomorrow? Breakfast is on me. Or lunch. Whatever you need, Ray.”

“I need my wife,” Ray said bitterly.

"But she's not coming back."

He turned around and walked away from Jenny, stumbling into another aisle. Chris had been watching from a distance.

"Who's that guy? He looks kind of suspicious."

Jenny told him about Bella.

"You girls will be careful, won't you? You had a narrow escape last time, Jenny."

"Don't worry, Chris. I'm not going up in a plane anytime soon."

"How can you joke about it?" Chris groaned.

"Did you hear about the Main Street project Barb Norton's undertaken?"

"We are at the far end so she hasn't given us much grief."

"Don't count on it," Jenny warned. "She came up with a big list for the café. I think she secretly wants to tear the place down."

"No way! The town can't function without the Boardwalk Café!"

"Shouldn't Barb know that? Wait till you meet her sidekick."

"You mean that girl who is going around snapping pictures?"

"She's put us on Instagram."

Chris whipped out his phone from his pocket.

"This I have to see."

"So we're giving the café a complete makeover. Can I count on you for some sweat equity?"

"As long as you pay me in donuts and cupcakes…"

"Heather said we can have a potluck, gather everyone."

"Now you're talking!" Chris grinned. "Better than risking your life playing detective."

"Bella Darling was barely twenty two, Chris. She didn't deserve such a gruesome end. I won't stop until I find out who did this to her."

Chapter 13

"I looked it up," Heather told Jenny on the phone. "It's in Baltimore."

Jenny had decided she needed to talk to the plane company Wayne had hired. Heather had managed to get the name from Crystal.

"You ready for a road trip?" Jenny asked.

"Oh yeah! Let's ask Molly. We can go shopping and have dinner at a city restaurant. It's been ages since I had some Thai food."

Plans were made and Saturday arrived soon enough. Jenny had secured an appointment at Eagle Aviation, a company that offered sky diving in the area. They also took special assignments like Wayne's where they arranged to fly people out to specific locations. The man Jenny spoke to thought she was booking a dive. She didn't want to tip him off prematurely.

"Do you have a list of questions ready?" Heather asked as they set off in Jenny's car.

Star was pitching in at the café so Jenny could take some time off.

"I mostly want to know if he saw Bella."

"Remember how she was dressed?

Would be hard to miss."

Molly spoke up from the back seat.

"If the pilot saw her, surely Wayne saw her too?"

"We'll see," Jenny said grimly.

Jenny followed the directions to a facility outside city limits. There was a big hangar at one end. A bunch of people dressed in colorful flying suits were avidly listening to an instructor.

"We are looking for Captain Jorge," Jenny told a man dressed in overalls.

He pointed her to a small trailer a few feet away.

Jenny, Heather and Molly trooped

toward the tiny structure. Jenny knocked on the door and went in.

"Captain Jorge? I'm Jenny King. We just talked on the phone."

"Hello ladies!"

An attractive older man greeted them cheerfully. His angular face was weather beaten. His close cropped hair had plenty of gray in it. Jenny thought of Tom Cruise in Top Gun and figured this is how he would have looked when he aged.

"Is this your first dive? We have some specials for first timers."

Jenny looked apologetic.

"Actually, we are not here for sky

diving."

The man frowned and waited for an explanation.

"We live in Pelican Cove. It's a small island off the coast of the Eastern Shore."

"Wait a minute. Isn't that where that country singer jumped?"

Jenny nodded. She was glad he had caught on quickly.

"We were sorry to hear about the girl. Are you related to her?"

"Not really," Jenny admitted. "But I am trying to find out what happened."

"Are you with the police?"

"No. I am doing this on my own."

"The police came here already. I talked to them."

"Can you spare some time for me, please? I just have a few questions."

Captain Jorge looked at his watch.

"I can give you half an hour. I have to take a group of ten up after that."

"You can take ten people up at a time?" Heather burst out. "I thought sky diving planes were really tiny."

"Some of them are," Captain Jorge said with a smile. "We have a larger aircraft here. I can take 20 people up at once."

"Did you have any other people on the

plane with Wayne Newman?" Jenny asked.

Jorge shook his head.

"They booked the whole plane. That's generally what they do for special events."

"You mean people sky dive to their wedding a lot?" Molly asked.

"You'd be surprised. Some people propose to their girl friends in the air." He shrugged. "More business for us."

"So you weren't surprised when Wayne Newman booked out your plane?" Jenny asked again.

"It's not that common," Captain Jorge

conceded. "It costs a small fortune."

"Wayne isn't hurting for money I guess."

"No ma'am."

"What's the usual process you follow for sky diving? Can you walk me through it please?"

"Most people go for a tandem dive. That's where we provide one of our own people to accompany you."

"Do they have a choice?"

"You need to be licensed if you want to do a solo dive. We make sure you have the right credentials."

"And Wayne Newman produced

them?"

"He sure did. He said he was going to do a tandem dive with his wife to be. He was going to take her down himself."

"Did he have his own parachute?"

"I guess. He was already rigged up when I saw him that day."

"Do you inspect the gear before the jump?"

"Of course," Captain Jorge said quickly. "We follow the necessary guidelines. If he rented one of our rigs, it must have gone through a quality check."

"Who was flying the plane that day?"

"I was. I'm the only pilot around here."

"Can you describe what happened?"

"The girl arrived when I was doing my flight checks. She was wearing a fancy wedding dress so I thought she must be the bride."

"Did she say who she was?"

Captain Jorge blinked, then shook his head.

"She told me she wanted to surprise her husband. Would I play along?"

"Then?"

"The way the plane is outfitted, there's hardly any room to hide. I put some stuff up there so she could crouch behind it and stay out of sight."

"What happened after that?"

"This guy arrived wearing a tux. He said his wife was afraid of heights. She wasn't coming after all."

"Go on."

"I played along. I figured the guy's going to get a nice surprise from his missus once we go up."

"When did he realize Bella was on the plane?"

"I don't know. I'm not sure."

"You must have heard them talk."

"We hit some unexpected turbulence. I wasn't really paying attention to them."

"What did you do after they jumped?"

"I realized the second chute didn't open. But there wasn't anything I could do at that point."

"Where do you keep the parachutes? Could someone have tampered with them?"

He waved his hand toward the hangar.

"There's plenty of people underfoot here all the time. I guess anyone could have done it."

"Do you have any security cameras?"

"Just one. The cops are going through the tapes."

"Could it have been an accident?"

"What do you mean?"

"Surely the parachutes have some wear and tear? Could it get ripped on its own?"

"Unlikely. If the chute is not packed properly, it can get stuck. But there's always the reserve."

"What's that?"

"It's a backup parachute," Captain Jorge explained. "If the main parachute is not open at a certain altitude, the backup opens. It's a lifesaver."

"But that didn't happen in this case," Jenny sighed.

"I heard it was turned off."

"Could that have happened accidentally?"

Captain Jorge shook his head.

"Anyone who values his life would never turn the reserve off. So no. And it doesn't get turned off on its own."

"So someone made very sure neither chute would open," Jenny pressed.

"Sure looks that way."

"Could Wayne have caught hold of her mid-air?"

"It depends on a lot of things," Captain Jorge said. "It's possible theoretically but it's not easy."

"Are you a sky diver too?" Jenny asked.

"Just curious."

"I am. But I'm also an overworked pilot. I hardly ever get to jump."

"Did you notice anything out of the ordinary that day?"

"That singer guy was sweating like a pig. Wedding jitters, I guess."

Wedding jitters, or a guilty conscience, Jenny wondered.

"Look, I have to go now," Captain Jorge said, glancing at his watch again. "Here's my card. Why don't you give me a call if you have any more questions."

The girls thanked the suave pilot and loitered around for a while.

"We should go sky diving some time," Molly said enthusiastically. "Looks like fun."

"Count me out," Jenny shuddered. "I'm twenty years too old for it."

One of the instructors looked up when he heard that.

"Age has nothing to do with it, lady. You need a strong will. Ain't nothing like that feeling, when you spread your arms up in the sky and feel the wind in your face."

"Sorry, but it's not my thing," Jenny said, thanking the man.

They piled into the car and drove into the city.

"Do you miss it?" Heather asked, as Jenny peered at the tall buildings and big shops.

"Not one bit," she smiled, honking her horn as a semi cut her off. "See that? Who needs that in life?"

Heather had looked up a Thai restaurant she wanted to visit. They ordered the largest mai tais and toasted their friendship.

"Ooooh, spicy!" Heather exclaimed, fanning her mouth as she dunked curry puffs into a sweet chili sauce.

"What did you think of Captain Jorge?" Molly teased. "Was he a hunk or what?"

"Molly Henderson! I saw how you were

staring at him."

"I'm single and unattached. I can look. Unlike you two."

"My divorce is final now," Jenny declared tipsily. "I'm as single as they come."

"What about the two men you've wrapped around your finger?"

"There's no such thing," Jenny muttered, sipping her cocktail through a straw.

"And Heather's with Chris. Let's not say any more."

"Until Chris pops the question, I am free to flirt with whoever I want to."

"Why don't you propose to him?" Jenny suggested. "It would be the scandal of the century in Pelican Cove."

"I know what you should do," Molly laughed. "Go sky diving with Chris and propose to him in the air."

There was a moment of silence and they all turned serious.

"What do you think Bella planned to do?" Jenny asked the girls.

"I think she wanted to ruin Crystal's wedding but it went horribly wrong."

"What if Bella messed with the parachutes? The bad chute could have been meant for Wayne but she wore it by mistake."

Jenny looked at Molly in shock.

"So you're saying she was the actual killer. But she ended up killing herself."

"It's possible," Molly protested. "Why wear a wedding dress at all? I think it was a ruse."

"How so?"

"She wanted to pass herself off as Wayne's bride. No one was going to stop a woman dressed like that. The sapphire must have been part of her disguise."

"I guess that makes sense," Jenny agreed.

"What if Wayne wanted Crystal out of the way? He booked the flight for the both of them, right? He could have messed with the parachute beforehand. But Bella wore it and jumped to her death."

"Who do you think Wayne was actually interested in?" Heather asked. "Crystal or Bella?"

"Maybe he was sick of them both," Jenny mused. "But chances are, he didn't want the baby."

"What baby?" Heather and Molly chorused.

Jenny told them about Bella's condition.

"Only a monster would kill his unborn child," Molly spat.

"We don't know who the father is," Jenny said.

"Do you think Crystal found out about the baby?" Heather asked. "She could have decided to get rid of Bella."

"But how did Crystal know Bella was going to be on the plane?" Jenny shot back.

"You're right," Heather sighed. "That doesn't make sense."

"What about that girl who talks to you?" Molly asked Jenny. "She knew Bella, didn't she?"

"Rainbow?" Jenny asked. "Are you saying Rainbow sent Bella up on that plane? But why?"

"It could have been a gag of some kind."

"Everyone I talked to said Bella was a sweet girl. I find it hard to believe she wanted to ruin Crystal's wedding."

"Nice girls don't have affairs," Molly argued.

"Surely Wayne must have noticed her on that plane?" Jenny asked. "What do you think?"

The girls had peeked into the airplane while Captain Jorge was doing some pre-flight checks.

"There's no way anyone could stay hidden in that space," Heather nodded.

"So Wayne Newman is definitely lying about something."

Chapter 14

"How was your trip?" Star asked Heather on Sunday morning. "Did you find out anything useful?"

"I am more confused than I was before," Jenny admitted, taking a big sip of her coffee.

"Why don't you write it down? It must be hard to keep it all straight in your head."

"You spoke my mind," Jenny told her aunt. "I made a rough sketch in a notebook last night. I couldn't sleep."

"Sketch?"

"Sketch may be the wrong word. I just wrote down the names of all the people and who they are connected with. You'd be surprised what the common thread is."

"Don't make me guess."

"Rainbow! She knew all of the players, except maybe Ray Fox. But I am thinking she might have known him too."

"Are you going to talk to her again?"

Jenny nodded.

"Be careful, okay?" Star cautioned. "I don't want you getting hurt."

"Relax! Rainbow's harmless."

"Not if she was mixed up in hurting that poor girl."

Jenny went to the café later than usual. Many people preferred to come for brunch on Sunday. Jenny made a batch of muffins and chopped fresh herbs for her scrambled eggs.

"You could plant herbs in your own patch out back."

Jenny recognized Mandy's voice but ignored her.

"Have you and Petunia gone through my list?"

"Don't you have someone else to pick on?" Jenny grumbled. "I'm busy."

"Some people have already started with their renovations," Mandy proclaimed. "We are painting park benches today. The curbs will be the last."

"We have a contractor coming in to give us an estimate," Jenny told her reluctantly.

"That's a step in the right direction," Mandy said approvingly.

Jenny called Heather at the inn.

"Fancy a trip to the country club?"

Heather had a headache.

"That's what too many mai tais will do to you," Jenny teased. "You need some solid food inside you."

"Don't mention food, please," Heather begged.

They drove to the club a couple of hours later. The first person they ran into was Wayne Newman.

"Ladies!" he greeted, tipping his hat at them. "Here to see Crystal?"

Jenny nodded vaguely. She didn't want to reveal the purpose of her visit.

"She's at the pool with her girls."

"What are they doing?"

"What they always do," Wayne shrugged. "I have no idea."

Jenny had a thought.

"We went to Eagle Aviation," she told

Wayne. "Got a tour of the place. We saw the plane you jumped from."

"It's one of the bigger ones," Wayne told them. "That's what I liked about the place."

"I thought the plane was really small," Jenny persisted. "It didn't even have a toilet."

Wayne looked uncomfortable.

"Most of the planes they use for sky diving don't."

"So here's my question," Jenny rushed ahead. "How is it possible you didn't see Bella before you jumped?"

Wayne turned red.

"I was excited. I didn't look around."

"You didn't see that big old white dress she was wearing?"

"Hey! It was my wedding day. I just wanted to get the dive over with so I could stand with my wife."

"You sound like you were doing it against your will."

Wayne clammed up after that.

"I got to go."

"Why did you challenge him like that?" Heather exclaimed as soon as Wayne was out of sight.

"I couldn't help it," Jenny said, shaking with anger.

"It changes nothing, except now he knows what we are thinking."

"Good. Maybe he'll slip up."

They went looking for Rainbow after that. One of the maids at the country club told them where her room was.

Rainbow looked a bit disheveled when she opened the door. She was wearing a silky robe and her hair was mussed. Jenny's nose twitched as she tried to smell something.

"Do you have a hangover too?" Heather laughed as they went in.

Rainbow stifled a yawn.

"There's not much to do here. I decided to sleep in."

"It's a beautiful day," Jenny said. "Don't they have a pool here?"

"Crystal and the girls are hanging out there," Rainbow said. "I couldn't take it anymore. I just want to go home."

"Do you know Ray Fox?" Jenny asked.

"Bella's husband? Sure."

"Do you know he's here in Pelican Cove?"

"I saw him in town."

"He seems lost without Bella."

"He loved her a lot."

"You know what I am thinking, Rainbow?" Jenny asked. "You seem to be the common thread here. You knew

Bella, you know Wayne and Crystal, you even know Ray Fox."

"What are you implying?"

"How do we know you didn't carry messages between these people?"

"You think I was spying on someone?"

"You could have. For example, you could have told Crystal about Wayne and Bella. Or you could have told Ray Fox about them."

"Why would I do that? Bella was my friend."

"That's what you told us before. But we heard that you were sworn enemies."

Rainbow rubbed her hands, pacing across the room.

"Who's feeding you this stuff?"

"Do you deny it?"

"There's someone else who knew Bella…"

Jenny's eyebrows shot up.

"Keep talking!"

"Crystal's mother. Why don't you go talk to her?"

"Don't worry, I will."

Jenny grabbed Heather's arm and they swept out of the room.

"Didn't you smell something familiar in

there?" she asked Heather.

Heather shook her head.

"Do you believe that girl?"

"She just wanted to get rid of us. But I know Crystal's mother lied to me. I want to talk to her again."

Kathy Mars was seated on the patio, sipping a frosty glass of lemonade. Her summer dress made her look ten years younger. She looked up at them with sparkling blue eyes the exact shade of the sunny skies.

"What brings you here, girls?" she asked. "Do you have any news for us?"

"Some," Jenny answered, choosing a chair opposite her.

Kathy poured some lemonade for them. She settled back in her chair and gave her a speculative look.

"Something's been bothering me since our last meeting," Jenny began. "You knew Bella Darling, didn't you?"

Kathy sighed, looking beaten.

"I met her a few times."

"Why did you keep that from me?"

"Bella and I didn't meet under the best of circumstances."

"Did you have a fight with her?" Jenny asked, sitting up.

"Nothing of that sort."

Kathy Mars gazed over the grassy

dunes.

"Crystal is so beautiful. I knew she was special right from the moment I held her for the first time."

Jenny didn't know if Kathy was going somewhere with her reminiscences but she didn't interrupt.

"I gave her the best of everything. When Crystal won a talent contest in junior high, I knew her future was in Hollywood."

"So you were a supportive mother."

"I planned her whole career. We had big plans, you know. Then we went to Hollywood."

"Wasn't it like you imagined?"

"It was everything we imagined and more. There was just one tiny problem. Everyone was beautiful and talented. Crystal needed something extra to stand out. I'm afraid she didn't have it."

"She didn't find any work?" Heather asked.

Kathy Mars snorted rudely.

"She got small roles. A cameo here, a music video there. We managed to get by but none of them were enough to launch her career."

"Until she landed the reality show," Jenny said flatly. "But she wasn't the first choice there too."

"Bella was the star of the show," Kathy said bitterly. "Crystal was one of the minor contestants. They wouldn't have kept her for more than one episode."

"What did you do?"

"I pulled in some favors. There was a scandal. Bella was off the show and Crystal was in."

"You managed that by yourself?"

"I had help. Money talks, Miss King. There are plenty of starving girls out there, ready to do anything for a bit of cash."

"Did you know Wayne Newman at that time?"

Kathy looked triumphant.

"That's where I scored a home run.

Bella was having an affair with Wayne Newman at the time. He seemed like a good fit for my Crystal."

"Did you pay him to go out with your daughter?"

"Give me some credit," Kathy Mars bristled. "I just arranged for them to meet accidentally a couple of times. I knew Wayne is a ladies' man. He fell under Crystal's spell."

"It didn't bother you that he might be cheating on your daughter?"

"My Crystal turned thirty this year. Her time's running out. She needed to tie the knot with someone influential and soon."

"I thought Crystal was the bigger star,"

Heather said.

"She is now," Kathy Mars said proudly. "Her star's been on the rise since she met Wayne. They are good for each other."

"What happened to Bella after you got rid of her?"

Kathy shrugged.

"I heard she had a husband. I figured she would be fine."

"Who helped you get rid of Bella?" Jenny asked.

"It doesn't matter now. Bella's gone."

"Was it Rainbow? Did she tell you some deep dark secret about Bella

Darling?"

Kathy Mars changed the subject and refused to divulge any more information.

Jenny stood up and stomped to Rainbow's room. Rainbow had showered in their absence. She was dressed in a pair of shorts and a bikini top.

"What do you want now?" she asked, rolling her eyes.

"You're a two faced liar, Rainbow!"

"What have I done?"

"You threw Bella under the bus, didn't you? Kathy Mars paid you off."

"I don't know what you're talking about."

"It's like I said, Rainbow," Jenny fumed. "You are the connection between all these people. Did you spy on Bella for Ray Fox? Did you tell him about the affair?"

"Look! I didn't ask him to come here, okay? I just saw him in town the night of the rehearsal dinner."

"What?" Heather and Jenny exclaimed.

"Are you sure you saw him the night before the wedding?"

Rainbow nodded.

"Crystal had sent me on an errand. I saw him go into that pub, what's it called?"

"The Rusty Anchor?"

"I guess. How many pubs do you have here anyway?"

"According to Ray Fox, he was back in L.A. when Bella fell to her death."

"No he wasn't," Rainbow shook her head. "He was right here in Pelican Cove."

"This doesn't let you off, Rainbow. You're up to something."

"Have you ever thought I might be a victim too?" she cried.

"Can you elaborate on that?"

Rainbow shut up after that.

"I'm going to the pool," she said, picking up a towel.

"Do you really suspect Rainbow?" Heather asked Jenny that afternoon.

They were watching the sunset from Star's porch, their feet up on the railing.

Jenny smacked her lips as she enjoyed the sundowners she had mixed for them.

"I didn't until now but I'm not sure any longer. She is definitely involved somehow."

"She could have told Ray Fox about Bella's affair. So he came here to confront her."

"Who told him Bella was here?" Jenny

mused. "Speaking of which, how many people knew Bella was in town?"

"How did we not know?" Molly asked, coming out with a plate of crab dip and crudités. "Crystal had booked out the entire country club for her wedding. And Bella wasn't staying at Heather's inn."

"She must have been staying out of town," Jenny said. "Someone would have noticed her otherwise."

"You think Kathy Mars stopped after paying Bella off?" Heather mused. "She seems awfully concerned about Crystal turning thirty."

"Turning thirty is a big deal," Molly stressed. "I remember how depressed I was on my thirtieth birthday."

"Rainbow turned out to be something else, didn't she?" Heather said, taking a sip of her drink.

"Each one of them is wearing a mask," Jenny said coldly. "I need to rip it off if I want to find out the truth."

Chapter 15

Jenny's room looked like a tornado had torn through it. The bed was strewn with discarded clothes, so was every available surface. Jenny had spent the past hour trying to find the perfect outfit for the annual Pelican Cove BBQ.

"Is this a big thing?" she had asked Star the previous evening.

"It happens once a year, so yes. The town goes all out. The men set up a smoker and start smoking the meat in the morning. The ladies make a ton of side dishes. And there's ice cream, of course."

"How many people go to this thing?"

"The whole town goes, Jenny. It's one of the highlights of the year."

"What about tourists?"

"We didn't allow tourists until recently. You know how the islanders are, but this year's going to be different."

"How so?"

"Barb Norton and her minion have butted in here too. They are going to charge admission and use the money for the town beautification."

Jenny was getting sick of Mandy James

and her brilliant ideas.

Star peeped into Jenny's room and started laughing.

"How old are you, girl? Sixteen?"

Jenny ignored her and held out two outfits. Star shook her head at either one of them.

"It's going to be hot as hell. I suggest you wear a swimsuit and a pair of shorts. You might want to take a dip in the ocean to cool off."

"Good idea!" Jenny said brightly.

The Boardwalk Café was closed for the day. Jenny was going to take advantage of it and enjoy her day. She wondered if she could spend some time with Adam.

"Adam will be there," Star told her, "but he might be on duty."

The two women set off for Main Street some time later. The aroma of smoking meat hit them as they made their way toward the drinks stand. Jenny picked up a paper cup of sweet tea and gulped it down. She was already feeling parched.

"There's Heather and Molly!"

She waved at her friends and hurried over.

A marquee had been set up in the middle of the street. People had brought their own trestle tables and camp chairs and set up wherever they found a spot. Betty Sue and Petunia sat on two plastic Adirondack chairs flanking a long metal table. A red checked table cloth barely covered it. Betty Sue had kept her knitting at home for a change. But her fingers twirled in a familiar rhythm.

Star sat on the chair Petunia had saved for her.

"Don't worry, I have a camp chair here for you too," Heather told Jenny.

The ladies caught up on the gossip for a while. The girls were dispatched to get some food.

"Isn't it too early?" Jenny asked.

"We have to pace ourselves," Heather explained. "I'm guessing you at least want to taste everything."

They were back with plates loaded with barbecued chicken, coleslaw and corn bread.

"The pork needs some more time," Molly told the older ladies. "We'll get baked beans and potato salad when we get the ribs."

"Hello beautiful!" a voice called out.

Heather and Jenny whipped their heads around making the others laugh. Jason and Chris were walking toward them.

"How's the barbecue?" Jason asked.

Chris and Jason were both wearing aprons proclaiming them to be pit masters. Sweat was pouring down their faces.

"You know how to operate a smoker?" Jenny asked Jason. "You are a man of many talents, Jason Stone."

He winked and whispered something in her ear, making her blush.

"What was that?" Betty Sue thundered.

Jason picked up a fork and started eating from Jenny's plate. Chris was eating a drumstick he had lifted off Heather's.

"Have you seen Adam?" Star asked Chris.

"He's on duty," Chris said. "He should be getting off soon though."

"This is not his kind of thing," Jason dismissed. "He'll probably pack a plate of food and go home."

"He's going to meet me here at 1," Jenny said sweetly.

Jason's face fell.

"Time to go back to the pit, buddy," Chris said to him.

"How much longer for the pork, boys?" Molly asked.

"We'll bring a plate for you when it's ready," Jason promised.

"Did you see his face?" Heather laughed when Jason was out of earshot. "There's going to be a battle here, Jenny, and you're the prize."

"Don't be silly," Jenny brushed her off.

"Jason is just a friend."

"A friend who takes you out on dates?" Molly teased.

"I see a lot of strangers around," Betty Sue commented. "I'm not sure I like that."

"You have to change with the times, Grandma," Heather consoled her.

"We cater to plenty of tourists year round," Betty Sue grumbled. "Isn't our whole business centered around tourists? The barbecue is supposed to be just for the town."

"Yoo-hoo…"

"Here's who you can thank, Betty Sue," Star said and Barb Norton came up to them, beaming from ear to ear.

Mandy tagged along a few steps behind.

"We're doing great," Barb told them enthusiastically. "Our take has already crossed five hundred bucks. You have Mandy to thank for this."

She paused and widened her eyes meaningfully.

"I'm sorry for taking over your town festival," Mandy James said cheerfully, sounding anything but sorry. "But we need funds, ladies. The town of Pelican Cove desperately needs some TLC."

"TLC?" Betty Sue asked. "Speak English, girl!"

"I mean, it needs a lot of repair."

"We were doing fine until you came along," Petunia snapped.

"I'm just doing my job, ladies," Mandy sighed.

"You better start looking for a new one soon," Betty Sue railed.

"We don't need a prize to tell us our town is pretty," Star added.

"You don't get it, do you?" Barb said, shaking her head. "That contest is going to boost business. It's going to bring in money. You can't stop progress, Betty Sue! Why don't you retire? Give your seat on the town board to Heather?"

Barb Norton stalked off with Mandy in tow.

"What does she care?" Petunia cried. "She doesn't even live here all year."

"How about a walk?" Heather asked Jenny.

There was a desperate look in her eyes. The girls knew where the conversation at the table was headed and they wanted no part of it.

They heard a buzz coming from one end of the street. A group of people was clustered together, pointing at something in the distance. The younger people had goofy looks on their faces. Some people were standing with their mouths hanging open.

"What's going on there?" Molly asked, putting on speed.

Crystal Mars and a bunch of her friends lay sunning themselves on the beach. The skimpiest of bikinis barely covered their honey colored bodies. Sunglasses larger than the bikinis covered their eyes.

"It's the invasion of the Barbies," someone in the crowd said.

"Look," a young acne faced boy chortled as one of the girls pulled off her bikini top.

An older woman, probably his mother, shielded his eyes with her palm.

"We thought this was a family friendly place," she said angrily.

Jenny and the girls walked down to the beach purposefully. Picking up some sarongs that lay in the sand, she flung them over the girls.

"What are you doing here, Crystal?"

"We thought we would get some barbecue."

"You need to cover up," Heather ordered. "There's a lot of kids around."

"But we're on the beach," one of the posse grumbled.

Jenny spotted Rainbow trying to smother a smile.

"Let me guess," Jenny said. "This was your idea."

"What's wrong with getting some sun?"

"Are you trying to create a scandal?"

"Relax," Crystal said lightly. "We get it."

She stood up and tied a sarong around her waist. She pulled the other one around her upper body and tied it around her neck. The other girls got up and copied her actions.

"Good enough?" Crystal asked. "Now where's this food everyone's talking about?"

"Ladies!" an authoritative voice called.

Jenny's heart skipped a beat as she recognized Adam's voice.

"There have been some complaints. This is not a topless beach."

"We're covered head to toe, Officer,"

Crystal said flirtatiously.

“So you are,” Adam nodded.

“Jenny’s been looking for you,” Heather spoke as Crystal and her posse walked up to the barbecue tent.

“No I haven’t,” Jenny protested.

“Can we go to your inn?” Molly asked Heather. “I need to freshen up.”

Heather and Molly started walking away, arm in arm.

“Molly? Heather?” Jenny called out. “I’m coming too.”

They ignored her and broke into a jog.

“I can hear them giggle, you know,” Adam said.

Jenny was feeling embarrassed. She wondered if Adam might lose his temper.

"Here we are!" he said softly.

"Are you still on duty?" she asked.

Adam looked at his watch.

"Only for the next five minutes."

"Do you want to get something to eat?"

Adam bobbed his head.

"I'm starving, Jenny. Let's go get some barbecue."

"We have a table somewhere in that big tent," Jenny told him as they stood in line. "The older Magnolias are over there."

"I was hoping we could sit somewhere else," Adam said. "Away from the crowd?"

"Hard to find an empty table," Jenny mumbled.

"I brought a mat," Adam told her. "We can sit on the beach."

They loaded their plates with the smoky meat. Jenny went for some baked beans and macaroni and cheese. Adam took a little bit of everything. They took their food out to the beach.

"We went to the sky diving company," Jenny told Adam. "The pilot mistook Bella for Crystal. That's why she was dressed in that bridal dress. It must have been her plan all along."

"I thought so too," Adam admitted. "Look, can we not talk about work?"

"Sure. What do you want to talk about?"

"Something more interesting," Adam grinned. "You."

"I don't have much to say," Jenny said, feeling a blush steal over her face.

"What's new with you, Jenny King?" Adam asked.

He picked an errant strand of Jenny's hair and tucked it behind her ear.

"How are the twins?"

"They are good. They were asking

about you."

"We might have to do some renovations at the café."

"Good," Adam said, looking into her eyes.

Jenny gulped and rubbed the heart shaped charm on her necklace.

"Adam," she said, struggling to find the right words. She didn't want to offend him. "Are we on a date?"

Adam didn't blink.

"When we go on a date, Jenny, you'll know."

"I didn't mean to…I wasn't…"

"I know you weren't," Adam assured

her. "Thank you for being so patient."

Jenny knew Adam had loved his wife a lot.

"Do you still miss her?"

"Sometimes I do," Adam said honestly. "I know it's been ten years. The girls are grown. What can I say, Jenny? She was my first love."

Jenny didn't have the same feelings where her ex-husband was concerned. He had dumped her for a younger model less than a year ago. The only thing Jenny felt when she thought of him was rage.

"You're too good, Adam."

"Are you sure you're talking about

me?" Adam joked. "I'm cranky and ill tempered most of the time. The younger guys at the station quake in fear when I walk by."

"You're kidding," Jenny laughed.

She picked up his hand and threaded her fingers through his.

"You've been through a lot, Adam. I can understand your frustration."

"One of these days, we will go out on a proper date," Adam promised. "How about taking a kayak out on the water?"

Jenny was deathly afraid of the water. But she didn't want to spoil the mood.

A hearty voice called out just then.

"Ahoy there!"

Jenny looked up to see Jason walking toward them with a tray loaded with food. Chris, Heather and Molly followed close behind.

"This is so not a date," Adam muttered, waving a hand at the new arrivals.

Chapter 16

Mandy James posted pictures of the town barbecue on Instagram. There was a sudden influx of tourists wanting to taste barbecue.

"We don't serve barbecue here," Jenny told a customer for the umpteenth time. "Can I get you a crab salad sandwich? We have Chesapeake Bay crabs, caught this morning."

Four hours later, she was finally ready to call it a day. Jenny thought of Adam on her way back home. She hadn't run into him since the barbecue.

Jason turned up for dinner with Chinese food.

"This is from my favorite restaurant on the mainland," he told them. "Just taste this Moo Shu Pork, Jenny. You'll love it."

"I don't mind some Lo Mein," Star said, dishing out a hefty serving with a pair of chopsticks.

"This is good," Jenny spoke between bites. "I'm so exhausted I can barely taste it though."

She massaged her feet with one hand while she spoke.

"Let me do that."

Jason gently picked up her foot and

placed it in his lap. He began giving her a foot massage. Star looked on approvingly.

"Stop it, Jason," Jenny groaned. "You're spoiling me."

"What are you doing Saturday night?"

"Soaking my feet in a big tub of water," Jenny sighed.

The heat and humidity were already getting to her.

"You need to hydrate more," Jason advised. "We should take a canoe out on the water one of these days. It will relax you."

"Err, I think not!"

"Jenny's scared of the water," Star spoke up. "Don't you remember that summer, Jason? All the kids decided to have an impromptu canoe race. Jenny stayed back on land to flag you off."

"Oh yeah!" Jason said, popping a dumpling in his mouth. "But that was years ago."

"Water's not my thing, Jason."

"So we'll do something else. Let's go to Virginia Beach Saturday night. There's a new club everyone's raving about."

"We'll see."

Jason agreed good naturedly. He was so amicable Jenny found it hard to deny him anything. He never lost his temper.

"Don't over think it," Star told her as they watched TV.

Jason had left long ago. He had to be in court first thing in the morning.

"He's nice, but I can't be serious about a lawyer. Not again."

"That's ridiculous. Just because one lawyer dumped you doesn't mean another will."

"I'm out of here," Jenny scowled.

She stepped out and started walking at a clip, barely stopping to look at the roses blooming at Seaview. She almost bumped into a body a while later.

"Jenny?" Adam's deep voice cut through the fog in her mind. "What's the matter?"

Tank put his paws on Jenny's shoulders and gave her a wet welcome.

"Hello sweetie," Jenny said, fondling the big yellow Lab. "I've missed you."

"He's missed you too," Adam said, leaning on his cane. "We've been busy."

"Find anything new?"

Adam shook his head.

"I'm not supposed to talk about this. We haven't confirmed the husband's alibi yet."

Jenny slapped her head and let out a tiny cry.

"I was going to tell you … he was here the day before the wedding."

"How do you know that?" Adam asked, grabbing her arm. "Are you sure about this?"

"Not really," Jenny said. "One of the bridesmaids told me. She said he went into the Rusty Anchor."

"We can easily verify that."

"How come no one at the pub came forward with this?"

Adam shrugged.

"Lots of tourists around these days. A stranger doesn't stand out so much."

"Have you interviewed this girl? She's

what would happen the next day.

Jenny was worked off her feet all morning. When the phone rang in the kitchen, she continued frosting a cupcake with one hand while she stuck the receiver in the crook of her neck.

Her mouth dropped open in shock when she heard the voice at the other end. The piping bag slipped from her hand and struck the floor, splattering frosting everywhere.

"How did this happen? I'm coming over."

Jenny hit the speed dial and called Heather.

"We need to go. Now!"

She was honking her horn in front of the inn ten minutes later. Heather came running out.

"Rainbow's dead."

"What?" Heather asked, getting in.

Jenny floored the gas pedal and the car took off with a screech of tires.

"Crystal just called the café. Rainbow didn't turn up for breakfast. They didn't think too much of it – she likes to sleep in sometimes. One of the girls knocked on her door when she didn't come out for lunch."

"What happened to her?"

"Some kind of overdose," Jenny spoke. "Sleeping pills, most probably."

They reached the country club soon after. Jenny remembered the building where Rainbow's room was situated. A bunch of police and emergency vehicles were parked outside.

Adam Hopkins frowned when he spotted Jenny.

"You can't be here, Jenny. This is a crime scene."

"What happened to her?"

"We don't know for sure yet. How did you find out about this?"

"Crystal called me."

Adam pointed toward the club house building.

"They are all over there. I think they were just about to have lunch. We are going to question all of them one by one."

"Can I sit in?"

"Of course not!"

"Did you talk to her since last night?"

"She was supposed to come in and meet me at 11."

They both knew Rainbow hadn't made it to the police station. Jenny had a hunch someone made sure about that.

She walked over to the dining room with Heather. Crystal sat on a chintz couch, clutching her mother's hand. Her eyes were red and her mascara had run down one cheek. A couple of girls sat squashed together in a big chair. One girl was pacing the room, burning a hole in the carpet.

"Jenny? Heather? Thank God you're here." Crystal sprang up and hugged Heather. "What's going on? Why is someone killing us off one by one?"

"We don't know what happened to Rainbow yet," Jenny said softly.

"She was such a sweet girl," Kathy Mars said in a sugary voice.

Kathy's expression didn't match her voice.

"We need to leave this place as soon as possible, honey."

Wayne Newman entered the room, holding his hat in his hand.

"Is it true?" he asked Crystal, looking crestfallen. "Is Rainbow gone?"

Crystal nodded, and a tear rolled down her eye.

Jenny wondered how much of it was authentic. If it was a performance, Crystal deserved the tag of reality star.

"Which one of you found her?" Jenny asked.

The girl who was pacing the floor spoke up.

"It was me. Rainbow liked to sleep in when she took one of her pills. I warned her not to take too many.

Maybe she took a double dose."

"You think this was an accident?" Jenny asked.

"She was so full of life," Crystal wailed. "And she had a good role in our new series. But her personal life was a disaster."

Jenny and Heather exchanged glances. They stayed quiet as if by an unspoken agreement.

"Wait a minute," Wayne Newman said. "What are you implying?"

Crystal let out another sob but said nothing.

"Let's not jump to conclusions," Jenny said quickly. "The police will tell us more."

Kathy Mars ordered some sandwiches and sweet tea and forced the girls to eat something. A couple of hours passed. Wayne Newman was sitting on the sofa next to Crystal. He caught Jenny's eye and motioned her to go outside.

Jenny stepped out on the long verandah facing the golf course.

"Have you made any progress?" he asked. "First Bella, now Rainbow. I'm beginning to think someone is targeting me."

Jenny stifled a laugh.

"You're alive and well, Wayne. How are you the victim here?"

"They were both my ladies," he said. "Crystal might be next."

"What does that mean?" Jenny asked. "Your 'ladies'?"

Wayne said nothing.

"You know Rainbow was sharing stuff with me?" Jenny asked.

"She was a bit greedy, but she had a good heart. She was feeling guilty about some things. I suggested she go talk to you."

"How long have you known Rainbow?" Jenny asked suspiciously.

"Long enough."

"Can you give me a straight answer?"

"I met Rainbow in Hollywood. We were both struggling at the time."

"I thought you knew her through Crystal?"

"Crystal wasn't on the scene at that time. At least, I didn't know her. Rainbow and I were an item."

Jenny let out a gasp. She hadn't seen it coming.

"Go on!"

"Bella became Rainbow's roommate later. I was famous on the music circuit by then. Bella fawned over me. What can I say, I fell for her."

"So you dumped Rainbow and went out with Bella?"

“I started going out with Bella, okay?”

“What went wrong?”

“They threw her off the set, I don’t know how or why. Crystal came into the picture. Before I knew it, we were going out.”

“But you continued seeing Bella behind Crystal’s back?”

“Bella and I were friends.”

“Friends with benefits, you mean.”

Wayne shrugged.

“I hate conflict. I like to live in harmony with everyone.”

“Do you mean you never break it off with your ex-girlfriends?”

"I don't see the need. Who knows when they might come in handy?"

Jenny struggled to stay calm.

"If you have any information about Rainbow, I suggest you give it to the police."

"She has a four year old son. He lives with her sister in Wisconsin."

"Rainbow had a son?" Heather cried. "Wasn't she too young?"

"None of these girls are as young as they say," Wayne said maliciously. "Bella was the real youngster among them. She was barely 22."

He looked genuinely sad when he said that.

"Do you know how to contact Rainbow's sister?"

Wayne nodded. He promised to give her contact information to the police.

He shook hands with Jenny and patted her on the shoulder. Jenny sprang back with a jerk. She had remembered something.

"What's that smell?" she asked. "Is it some kind of perfume?"

"I don't wear perfume," Wayne said, bewildered. "Just aftershave."

"You scumbag! You were still getting it on with her, weren't you?"

Wayne was quiet.

"You were in Rainbow's room the other day," Jenny accused. "Don't try to deny it."

"Like I said … we go way back."

"You were carrying on with her right under Crystal's nose?" Heather gasped. "Weren't you afraid of getting caught?"

"What's Crystal gonna do? She's so desperate to get married, she'll look the other way no matter what I do."

"Why are you marrying Crystal?" Jenny asked. "Do you love her at all?"

"I loved Bella for a while, and I loved Rainbow. Crystal is just good for the ratings."

Kathy Mars stood in the doorway with

a vicious look in her eyes. Jenny was sure she had heard the last bit. Kathy's lips stretched into a horrible smile.

"Why don't you come in? I just called for lemonade."

Chapter 17

Jenny, Heather and Molly walked to the Rusty Anchor one evening.

"Is Chris meeting us there?" Molly asked Heather.

Memorial Day had come and gone. The café had been flooded with tourists eager to taste the cupcakes and crab salad they had seen on Instagram. Mandy James had done them a favor after all.

A team of contractors and volunteers was busy making small changes on Main Street. The town was beginning to look spiffy.

"Don't these look pretty?" Heather asked, pointing toward some new flower beds that had sprung up by the side of the road. "I don't know, Molly," she pouted. "I don't keep tabs on him."

"Trouble in paradise?" Jenny asked.

They found a lot of familiar faces at the Rusty Anchor. Jimmy Parsons waved at them from the bar. Jenny got up to say hello to him. Jimmy had apparently been at it for some time.

"How's your aunt, little lady?" he asked.

Jenny had guessed Jimmy had a thing for her aunt.

"Why don't you come over for dinner sometime, Jimmy?"

Jimmy nodded happily. "I could use a home cooked meal. You're a good girl, Jenny."

Jenny spotted a familiar figure seated at the other end of the bar.

"What is Ray Fox still doing here?" she asked the girls when she went back to their table.

Jason Stone had joined them in her absence.

"You remember he's my client, Jenny? I can't talk about him."

"Haven't the police cleared him yet? Why is he still hanging out in Pelican

Cove?"

"My lips are sealed," Jason stressed.

"What if he wants to talk to me?"

Jenny walked over to where Ray was seated. She pulled up a stool and climbed up on it.

"Hello Ray. Remember me?"

Ray Fox looked at her with bloodshot eyes. He nodded and took another sip of his drink.

"How long have you been in town really?"

"Am I busted?" he asked.

"Yes, you are. You were seen here the day before Crystal's wedding."

"Did that old roommate of Bella tell you this?"

"She may have."

"What's it matter to her? She's got to stop meddling in my business."

"You don't have to worry about her."

"Why not? She always had it in for Bella. Did you know she got Bella thrown off the set? My Bella lost the role of a lifetime because of that girl."

"You must have been mad at her."

"You bet I was. We both were."

"Is that why you killed her?"

Ray straightened and blinked at Jenny in confusion.

"What are you talking about?"

"That girl – Rainbow – she was found dead a few days ago."

"You've got to be kidding me."

"I'm not. How did you not hear about this?"

"Nobody told me…"

So Ray Fox had a possible grudge against Rainbow. Jenny decided to talk to Adam about it later.

"Why did you come here, Ray? Did you know Bella was planning something for Crystal's wedding?"

"Look, I don't care one bit about Crystal Mars, okay?"

Jenny folded her hands and waited for him to continue.

"I found out Bella was seeing Wayne Newman again."

"Who told you that?"

"I had my sources…never mind how I found out…people talk."

"So you came here to confront Bella and kill her?"

"Why would I kill her? Bella was the love of my life."

Ray's eyes filled up as he spoke. Jenny wondered if she was witnessing another stellar performance. It was hard to tell.

"Sure! You loved Bella even though she

was cheating on you."

"Bella was beautiful and she had a heart to match. She had a string of admirers wherever she went. But she never slipped. Until she ran into Wayne Newman again …"

"What was special about Wayne? From all accounts, he's a womanizer."

"She never got over him."

"You knew about Bella and Wayne before you got married?"

Ray Fox took a big gulp of his drink.

"Bella promised me it was all over. We were very happy for a while. Then I had to go on location for a few months."

"She ran back to Wayne?"

"It wasn't like that. She met him at some awards function. He was engaged to Crystal. Bella hated Crystal. I think she went out with Wayne just to spite Crystal."

"Looks like that backfired."

Ray smiled mirthlessly.

"She got caught up in him again."

He looked at Jenny, struggling with what to say next.

"I know about the baby," Jenny said gently.

Ray wiped his eyes with the back of his hand.

"She thought it was the end. She rushed over here to confront Wayne. She wanted to beg him to marry her."

"What about you?"

"She thought I would dump her."

"So she didn't trust you, huh?"

"Bella was so young," Ray sobbed. "She ran away from home at sixteen. People only took from her. She had been treated like crap by most people in her life."

"She assumed you would do the same."

"That's my fault, I guess. She didn't trust me. I failed to make her believe."

"She was just insecure."

“She shouldn’t have been. She was my wife. It was my job to look after her no matter what.”

“How did you know she was coming here?”

“I was out of town when Bella got on the plane. I came in to Los Angeles the same evening. She had left a print of her ticket on the coffee table.”

“Was that her way of letting you know where she was?”

“I think it was a cry for help.”

“What did you do then, Ray?”

“I got the next flight out and came here.”

"Bella wanted to break it off with you so you messed with her parachute. Is that right?"

"That's a lie!"

Jenny wondered if she had pushed him a bit too far.

"Bella and I met. We talked about everything. She told me about the child. I didn't mind who the father was. We could raise it as our own."

"Really? You are that noble?"

"I had an accident years ago," Ray confessed. "I can't have kids. We had talked about adoption or sperm donation. This felt like a blessing to me."

"What about Wayne?"

"He could do as he pleased. If he wanted to be a part of the child's life, we would have come to some agreement."

"But didn't Bella come here to disrupt the wedding?"

"She just wanted to talk to Wayne. She had high hopes from him."

"But you decided to raise the child together. Why did she go up on that plane then?"

"That's what I can't figure out," Ray blubbered.

Jenny gave him some time to collect himself.

"You really don't know why she went up in that plane?"

"I had no idea she was going to do that. We were flying back home later that day."

Ray Fox didn't meet Jenny's eyes while he said it.

"You're hiding something, Ray. What is it? Maybe I can help you if you are honest with me."

Ray hesitated.

"She said she had one last thing she needed to take care of."

"So she was going to confront Wayne after all."

"I don't know," Ray said, sounding helpless. "Maybe I should have guessed she would do something silly."

"Could she have wanted to cause a stir at the wedding?"

"Bella wasn't vindictive," Ray said firmly. "And it was Wayne's wedding too. She wouldn't do that to him."

"Something or someone made her go up there," Jenny said, "with a faulty parachute."

"Bella's a pro at sky diving. She would never go up there without checking her rig."

"She must have trusted whoever handed it to her."

feelings about her cheating ex-husband. She didn't have a single kind thought about him in her mind. Was Ray Fox for real, she wondered. Or was he putting on a big act.

"Let's hope the police solve this case soon."

"Weren't you going to find out what happened?"

"I can't promise anything," Jenny said honestly. "I'm not a trained investigator. I just talk to people and stumble on the truth."

"Don't be so modest. I heard how you solved a stranger's murder a few months ago."

"Is there anything else about Bella that

you can tell me? Did you find out anything about her family, for instance?"

"I told you, they disowned her long ago," Ray told her. "I'm all she had."

"Let me know if you remember anything," Jenny stressed. "You can find me at the Boardwalk Café."

Jenny went back to her table after that. Chris had joined them in her absence, along with an unwelcome guest.

"What do you want, Mandy?" Jenny snapped.

Mandy James looked hurt.

"I'm just having a drink with my new friends."

The town had issued an ordinance against the Boardwalk Café that day, ordering them to undertake all the repairs suggested by the beautification committee.

"Friends don't throw each other under the bus."

"You're talking about the letter."

"How'd you guess?"

"Relax, Jenny," Jason said, placing an arm around her shoulders and making her sit. "You're breathing fire. She's just doing her job."

"Exactly!" Mandy exclaimed. "How can you not understand that, Jenny? It's not personal."

"Petunia's blood pressure is up from the stress. That's how personal it is to me."

Mandy stood up and bid goodbye to everyone.

"I know where I am not wanted."

"What was that?" Molly asked. "You could at least have been polite."

"We got the contractor's estimate today," Jenny told her friends. "It's five figures. Five figures!"

"I thought we were pitching in to help?" Chris asked.

"That's just the contractor's work. We will still need you all to help, and we'll need to spend more on paint and other supplies."

"Stop worrying about that for a moment," Jason soothed. "Did you make Ray talk?"

"He's either a very good actor or he's innocent."

"We are here to relax," Heather reminded her. "No more talk of the café or anything unpleasant."

Chris and Jason called for a fresh round of beer. Eddie Cotton brought over their pints on a tray, along with a bowl of potato chips.

"There's one extra," Jenny laughed as she picked up her mug.

Eddie pointed toward the door. Adam

Hopkins had just walked in.

"Hello, slacker!" Jason greeted him. "Is the police department going to survive without you tonight?"

Heather whispered something to Molly and they both started to giggle. Jenny guessed it was something about her. She ignored them and pulled up another chair for Adam.

Wedged between Jason on one side and Adam on another, Jenny rubbed the small gold heart hanging on a chain around her neck. She liked them both for different reasons. She might have to choose between them one day but she was in no hurry to do so.

Chapter 18

The high school students Petunia had hired started working at the café. Jenny spent a couple of days showing them the ropes. She hoped they would be more help than hindrance.

There was a tinkling laugh and Jenny looked up to see Crystal and her posse enter the café. They wanted to sit out on the deck.

"Hello Jenny." Crystal hung back to talk to her. "Found anything new?"

Jenny shook her head.

“I’m trying. What are you gals doing out here in town?”

“We got cabin fever,” she replied, making a face. “And I was craving your cupcakes. Got anything new?”

“I just finished frosting a new batch of cupcakes with raspberry and Grand Marnier frosting. I’ll bring them out.”

Jenny put a pitcher of icy lemonade and her cupcakes on a tray. She remembered how Rainbow had talked to her the last time the girls visited the café.

“Anything new on Rainbow?” she asked Crystal.

“The police confirmed she died of an overdose.”

According to Jenny, it had either been intentional or an accident. She couldn't imagine Rainbow taking her own life. She was too much in love with herself.

The girls started talking about Rainbow, saving Jenny the need to ask any probing questions.

"She was so happy about her new role," one of the girls said. "It was all thanks to Crystal."

Crystal blew an air kiss at the girl.

"We're going to need someone else to fill that spot now."

"First Bella, now Rainbow," another girl spoke up. "I think the show's jinxed. Who knows, any one of us could be next."

"You remember what happened on the third season of that show we were on?"

The girls plunged into a discussion about the different times they had encountered bad luck.

Jenny went in, tired of listening to their chatter.

"They are a bunch of idiots," Crystal said, following her into the kitchen. "All that matters is the ratings."

"Have your ratings suffered?"

"They are at an all time high," Crystal beamed. "That's the thing about them, Jenny. They shoot up in good times and bad. They are based on the amount of interest the show generates, you know? The company is playing up

Rainbow's death. Fans are lining up to place flowers and teddy bears outside the studio back home."

"I didn't know Rainbow was that popular," Jenny remarked. "Wasn't she like a supporting actress?"

"Not even that," Crystal sighed. "But she's got a big following now. It's like the authors who become famous posthumously."

"That's good for your show. You must be happy."

Crystal rolled her eyes.

"It might be good for the show in the short term. But it's not good for me. I am the star of this show, not Rainbow."

Jenny decided that ruled Crystal out as a suspect. She would never do anything to endanger her position as queen bee.

"How was she when you talked to her last?"

"I don't remember. She was her usual self, I guess. She was closer to my mother than me."

"She was friendly with Wayne too, I hear."

"What are you implying, Jenny?"

"Nothing! I'm saying Rainbow was a friendly soul. She was quite chatty."

"Really? What did you talk about?"

"Nothing in particular."

Crystal stifled a yawn and went back to her table. The girls lingered for a couple of hours and ordered lunch.

One of the starlets stepped into the kitchen with a list of special instructions.

"One crab salad sandwich without tomato, one crab salad without mayo and one crab salad sandwich without bread, please."

"The crab salad without mayo will take time," Jenny told her. "You want to wait here while I mix a new batch?"

The girl sat down at the kitchen table.

"How well did you know Rainbow?" Jenny asked her.

"Not very well," the girl admitted. "She didn't hang around with us much."

"Oh? But I thought she was part of Crystal and her group of friends."

"She was a bit older than us, and more experienced."

"You mean she was a senior actress?"

The girl looked over her shoulder and leaned forward.

"Don't tell anyone I said this, but she was a better actor than Crystal."

"Why didn't she get the lead role then?"

The girl shrugged.

"Talent is not the only requirement…"

"Did she get along with everyone?"

"She was nice to everyone but she kept her distance."

Jenny pursed her lips as she asked the next question.

"You don't think anyone had a grudge against her?"

The girl grew uncomfortable.

"Some of the girls were a bit jealous," she finally admitted. "Other than Crystal, Rainbow was the only one who had her own room, see? The rest of us have to share a room."

"How did she manage that?"

The girls shrugged.

"She was pretty friendly with Kathy. Crystal's Mom, you know."

The girl's voice dropped to a whisper.

"And she was friendly with Wayne."

Jenny knew the nature of Rainbow's friendship with Wayne very well. She didn't contradict the girl.

"Did she come to dinner the previous night? When was the last time you saw her?"

"Rainbow didn't join us for dinner. She said she had some personal business to take care of."

"Yeah? Like what?"

"She didn't say. But I saw her drive out

of the club around six."

Jenny whirled around to look at the girl. So Rainbow had probably visited someone in town.

"Was that the last time you saw her?"

"Kind of. I saw Wayne coming out of her room later that night. He was saying something. He must have been talking to her, right?"

"What time was this?"

"I don't remember. But it was late."

Jenny thought of the void Rainbow's death had created.

"Was there anyone who was angling for Rainbow's role?"

"Almost everyone was," the girl laughed. "Our roles are scripted beforehand but anything is possible on a reality show. If someone works up a fan following, the producers can keep them on longer, fire someone else."

"So you're trying to be one up on each other all the time?"

"I guess." The girl shrugged.

Jenny decided she would never be able to handle that kind of tension.

"Must be hard on you. Aren't you all friends?"

"We are friends up to a point. But we also need to look out for ourselves. Everyone knows that. There are no hard feelings."

Jenny thanked the girl and promised she would bring over the special orders to their table. She spent the rest of the day thinking over what the girl had said. She needed to talk to Wayne Newman again.

Petunia came in to clean up an hour later.

"Are you going home to change?"

"Change for what, Petunia?"

"Have you forgotten? They are unveiling the new welcome sign. There's going to be a ribbon cutting and a special guest."

"Let me guess. Mandy James is behind all that."

Petunia nodded.

"And you still want to go?"

Petunia sat down with a sigh.

"I know Mandy's been hard on us. But this is about the town. We have been talking about getting a new welcome sign for years."

"In that case, lead me on…"

"Aren't you going to change? The whole town will be there."

Petunia widened her eyes when she said 'whole town'.

"Do we have enough time?"

"It's at five. You will have to hurry."

"Do you want me to pick you up?"

"Thanks dear, but I am riding with Heather and Betty Sue."

Jenny and her aunt drove to the venue in time for the event. The sign was erected a quarter mile before the bridge that led to the island of Pelican Cove. Jenny was surprised to see Wayne Newman standing next to Barb Norton and Mandy James. There were a bunch of reporters clicking pictures like crazy.

It turned out Wayne Newman was going to cut the ribbon and unveil the new sign. He did that with a grin and pulled off the white cloth covering the sign. Then he gave a small speech.

Mandy James thanked everyone for coming and thanked the artist who had created the sign. Star looked stoic while she took it all in.

Wayne caught Jenny's eye and pulled her to a side.

"I couldn't say no," he explained. "That Mandy chick is pretty persuasive."

"I know," Jenny agreed.

She nodded toward the reporters.

"Looks like the paparazzi know where you are now."

Wayne shrugged.

"I've been below the radar long enough. It's time to go home. Maybe the media will put some pressure on the police."

"You lost two friends in a short period of time, Wayne. I am sorry for your loss."

Wayne curled his fingers.

"They were both good people. I know I was seeing all of them at once. But I really cared for Bella and Rainbow."

Once again, Jenny wondered if someone was killing off Wayne's lady loves one by one. Was Crystal in danger too?

"When was the last time you saw Rainbow?"

"I spent some time with her that afternoon."

"Did you arrange to meet her away

from the club?"

"Why would I do that, Jenny? I could meet her there any time I wanted to."

So Rainbow hadn't left the club to meet Wayne. Had she just gone out for a drive?

"Someone saw you coming out of Rainbow's room that night."

Wayne looked guilty.

"I looked in on her later that night," he admitted reluctantly. "I liked to spend some time with her before turning in."

He gave Jenny a meaningful look making her blush.

"You didn't go to Crystal before

turning in?"

"I did. I went to Rainbow first."

Jenny tried to hide her disgust. Then she told herself she wasn't the moral police.

"Was she in her room?"

Wayne looked flustered again.

"She was fast asleep. I shook her but she wouldn't wake up. I thought she might have taken one of her pills."

Wayne could have given her the pills himself. Why would he do that though, Jenny asked herself.

"Were you talking to yourself when you left her room?"

"I was talking to her," Wayne said sheepishly. "I thought she might be play acting."

"And why would she do that?"

"We had a fight earlier that day," Wayne confessed. "She told me she didn't want to see me again."

Jenny put her hands on her hips and glared at Wayne.

"When were you going to tell me that?"

Wayne ran a hand through his hair.

"Rainbow's dead. How would it look if I admitted we argued on the day she died?"

"It looks bad," Jenny nodded. "But

hiding it looks worse."

"I could've done something, Jenny," Wayne cried suddenly. "I could have saved her."

"You didn't know what was wrong with her."

"So what? If I had raised an alarm, got a doctor to look at her, maybe she would be with us right now."

Wayne's distress seemed genuine enough. But Jenny had her doubts.

"What time did you go to her room, Wayne?"

"Around nine? It was a little past that, I think."

"Did you visit her at the same time every night?"

"Not exactly. We would meet at dinner and then decide if we were going to see each other later that night."

"Where did you go after you came out of Rainbow's room?"

"I went to see Crystal."

"Did you tell her about Rainbow?"

Wayne shook his head.

"I think you should tell all this to the police."

Wayne didn't look too happy about the suggestion.

"Do I have to? I think they already

suspect me."

Jenny didn't want to comment on that.

"If you're innocent, you should volunteer any information you have, Wayne. Hiding anything, even the smallest detail, makes you look suspicious."

"I'll think about it," Wayne promised.

Mandy came and took Wayne away for a photo session. Jenny saw her coax people into standing on either side of the new sign. She turned around at a familiar voice.

Adam Hopkins stood a few feet away, holding Tank's leash. Tank barked a welcome as soon as he saw Jenny.

"Meddling in police business?" Adam asked with an inscrutable expression.

Chapter 19

The Magnolias were enjoying their usual mid-morning break at the Boardwalk Café. Jenny had been busy getting their new hires up to speed. Petunia had convinced Jenny to let the kids manage the front desk. Jenny was taking a much deserved break.

"What's on your mind, girl?" Betty Sue asked, her hands busy knitting a lime green scarf. "You look like someone stole your candy."

That produced a laugh out of everyone.

"She's been like that for a while," Star told them. "I can't get a smile out of her."

"Are you still thinking about Bella?" Heather asked.

Jenny gave a slight nod.

"What do the police say?" Betty Sue asked. "Haven't you talked to that Hopkins boy recently?"

"The police haven't made any arrests," Jenny told them. "And they are not holding anyone."

"So they are clueless," Molly stated. "What does Adam say?"

Jenny flared up when she heard Adam's name.

"Why would Adam say anything?" Her chest heaved with emotion. "You know he never tells me anything. He hasn't given me a single update on what's happening."

"Are those film people still in town?" Molly asked.

"They are here till the end of the week," Heather informed them. "I spoke to Crystal yesterday."

"And they won't be coming back!" Jenny exclaimed. "How can the cops let them leave?"

"They stuck around long enough," Heather argued. "They all have deadlines. The show has lost a lot of money, it seems. The studio's lawyers are putting a lot of pressure on the authorities here."

"I'm surprised the police haven't charged anyone yet,' Jenny said nastily. "It's not as if they need proof."

An old incident still rankled. Her aunt had been found guilty of murder by the local police earlier that year. The police had latched on to her without any evidence. Jenny had stood by her aunt and worked hard to find the real killer.

"This is a high profile case," Molly said. "They will think twice before pointing the finger at anyone."

"How do you know so much about this?" Petunia asked Molly.

"Jason told me that," she admitted.

"Jason," a trio of voices chorused. "When did you meet Jason?"

"I ran into him at the bakery," Molly snorted. "It's not like we went on a date or anything, Jenny."

"I don't mind," Jenny shrugged. "You can go out with Jason if you want to."

"We all know Jason's sweet on you," Molly laughed.

"Forget about Jason," Star said. "What are you thinking about, Jenny? Do you have any ideas about who might have done this?"

"Is it one person or two?" Heather asked.

"I think the two deaths are related,"

Molly said. "Both the girls knew each other, didn't they?"

"What do you think, Jenny?" Betty Sue thundered, pausing her hands for a second.

"I don't know. I keep going around in circles."

"I told you, Jenny," Star said. "You need to write it all down."

"I think Wayne's our guy," Molly said. "He's too good looking."

"That's not a crime, honey," Star said.

"Being a womanizer is, isn't it?" Molly asked.

"I don't think so," Jenny said,

scrunching up her face in thought. "He's not married yet."

"It's immoral for sure," Molly said stoutly.

"I agree with that," Petunia supported her. "So this Wayne guy is engaged to one girl, and he was carrying around with two other girls."

"He's so nice about it," Heather sighed.

"Of course he's nice!" Molly snapped. "He gets to have his cake and eat it too."

"Not any longer," Jenny reminded them.

"What do you think about Wayne?" Star asked her.

"He's a bit of a bad boy," Jenny admitted. "But he seems nice."

"That's exactly how he gets all the girls to fall for him," Molly laughed. "You too, Jenny?"

"I can't forget he was up there with Bella," Jenny spoke up. "How could he not have seen her?"

"How many people knew that poor girl took sleeping pills?" Petunia asked.

"Almost everyone, it seems," Jenny said, flinging her hands in despair.

"Why would she take an overdose?" Heather asked. "Surely someone must have forced her?"

"Why didn't she make any noise or

something?" Molly asked.

"It's no use," Jenny grumbled. "I've asked myself these same questions plenty of times."

"Is Wayne the only one you suspect?" Star asked.

"We can't forget Ray Fox was in town too," Jenny said.

"That's Bella's husband?" Betty Sue asked.

Molly spoke up.

"You think Ray would want to kill her because of the child?"

"He gave me a pretty tall story about wanting a child," Jenny mused. "But it's possible it was a bluff. Maybe he wanted revenge."

"Why would he come all the way to the east coast for that?" Heather asked. "Surely he could have done it when Bella got back home?"

"What if Bella managed to convince Wayne to marry her?"

"That doesn't make sense, Jenny. Bella was married to Ray. She would have gone back home no matter what Wayne said to her. Ray Fox had plenty of opportunity to get even with her once she went to L.A."

"Doing the deed here is like pointing the finger at himself," Molly added. "Surely he's not that stupid?"

"Ray might have been angry at his wife," Star said. "What did he have against Rainbow?"

"Rainbow was the one who introduced Wayne and Bella," Jenny explained. "He could have had a grudge against her for that."

"So he killed her for an old grudge?" Star asked. "That doesn't make sense."

"Why would Wayne kill Rainbow then?" Jenny asked. "He actually liked her. And she was his girl friend."

"What if Rainbow knew what Wayne did to Bella? She decided to spill the beans?" Molly was very happy with her idea.

"She could have threatened to tell

Crystal about Bella," Heather suggested.

"After Bella was gone?" Jenny asked. "I am sure Crystal already knew about Bella and Wayne. She said she didn't care about Wayne's character."

"Saying it is one thing, dear," Petunia spoke up. "No woman is going to like the fact that her man is carrying around with someone else."

Jenny thought of Wayne's final visit to Rainbow. She hadn't mentioned it to anyone.

"I'm going to talk to Adam," she declared, standing up suddenly. "I just thought of something."

"Go on then…" Betty Sue cackled.

The older ladies exchanged knowing glances as Jenny sped down the café steps to the boardwalk. She hurried toward the police station which was a couple of blocks down the road.

A few minutes later, she was standing in front of Adam Hopkins with her hands on her hips.

"We need to talk, Adam!"

"What is it, Jenny? I am busy."

"I have some questions about Rainbow."

"That's an ongoing investigation. You know I can't tell you anything about it."

"Even if it might help you solve the case?"

Adam folded his arms and leaned back in his chair.

"One question."

"When did Rainbow die?"

"Any time after 8 PM. Between 8 and midnight is the best guess."

"So she was already dead…" Jenny mumbled to herself.

"What's that?" Adam asked. "Are we done here?"

"She must have been gone when Wayne visited her that night."

"Wayne Newman went to see Rainbow the night she died?" Adam asked incredulously. "How do I not know that?"

"One of the bridesmaids told me," Jenny revealed. "I asked Wayne about it."

"He could have given her the pills," Adam said, incensed.

"Why would she willingly take an overdose?"

"She was in love with this Wayne guy, wasn't she?" Adam asked.

"Wayne's taking it hard."

"It could be an act. I need to talk to Wayne Newman about this."

"He'll probably come to you himself," Jenny told him.

She sat down and pulled at the chain around her neck.

"Did you find out where Rainbow went that day?"

It was yet another fact Adam was not aware of.

"Someone must have seen her in town," Adam said hopefully. "We will start questioning people."

"She could have just gone to the Rusty Anchor for a drink."

"It's all speculation at this point," Adam sighed.

"Did you find any other clues in her room?"

"Yes, Jenny. We found a note telling us who killed her."

"You don't have to be nasty, Adam!"

Adam hid a smile and leaned forward. He clasped Jenny's hand in his.

"You're so cute, Jenny," he said hoarsely.

Jenny wasn't sure she liked being referred to as cute.

"Do you mean stupid?"

"No, I mean cute," Adam insisted, still holding her hand.

Jenny wriggled out of his grip and stood up.

"I have to get back to the café."

Jenny felt flustered as she walked back to the café. Adam had never held her hand before. Spotting an empty bench on the boardwalk, she sat down and stared at the sea. Was Adam beginning to respect her sleuthing abilities or was he just humoring her. Whatever the reason, Jenny decided she liked holding hands with him.

Chaos reigned back at the café. The two new kids had managed to mix up the orders. Jenny redid a dozen orders while Petunia went around pacifying their regular customers.

"Are you ready for lunch?" Petunia asked her a couple of hours later. "Better eat something before we prep for tomorrow."

"Let's make scones for breakfast,"

Jenny suggested as she speared some grilled chicken on her fork.

It was the special of the day, made with dried cranberries, strawberries and almonds. Jenny added an orange thyme dressing that was very popular with locals and tourists alike.

"We haven't baked any in a while," Petunia agreed. "Let me ask Betty Sue if she wants a batch at the inn."

The phone rang just as Petunia stood up to call Betty Sue.

"It's for you," she told Jenny, handing her the receiver.

The old fashioned wall phone in the kitchen had a long cord so Jenny could stay seated while she grabbed the handset.

"Hello?" she said tentatively, raising her eyebrows at Petunia.

"Hello, Ms. King," a vaguely familiar voice crackled on the line. "This is Jorge, from Eagle Aviation? You were here a few days ago…"

"Captain Jorge!"

"I hope you don't mind the intrusion."

Jenny felt a burst of excitement as the handsome old pilot's face swam before her eyes. Had Captain Jorge remembered something about Bella?

"Not at all," she hastened to assure him. "How can I help you, Captain?"

"I wonder if you can pass on a message?" he asked hesitantly.

"Of course. What is it?"

"A young girl came to meet me here a couple of days ago. She was staying at the Pelican Cove Country Club. She mentioned knowing you."

"Who was it?"

"I can't recollect the name," Captain Jorge apologized. "It was something exotic. She was tall and blond with violet eyes, quite attractive if you don't mind my saying so."

Jenny's chair toppled to the floor as she stood up suddenly.

"Was it Rainbow? Was that the girl's

name?"

"That's it!" Captain Jorge's relief was palpable. "She came here just as we were winding down for the day."

"What did she want?" Jenny asked, holding her breath.

"She wanted to book a dive," Captain Jorge explained. "She had a lot of questions. I handed over the FAQs we print out for first timers. Then she said she had safety concerns."

"What kind of concerns?"

"She wanted to know what happened if she brought her own rig. That's the parachute…would someone still check it out before she went up?"

"And what was your answer?"

"We don't check personal rigs," Captain Jorge said immediately.

"But I thought you said you had strict quality checks?" Jenny probed. "Didn't you mention some kind of guidelines?"

"We do that for our own gear," Captain Jorge explained. "We don't touch your gear. People who bring their own parachutes sign a waiver. We are very meticulous with our paperwork, Ms. King."

Jenny figured the company was just making sure they were not liable.

"I understand," Jenny said. "What was the message, Captain Jorge?"

"She booked a dive for tomorrow evening but she didn't leave any contact information. I just wanted to confirm she's still coming as scheduled?"

Jenny swallowed a lump as her fingers tightened around the telephone cord.

"You should cancel that appointment, Captain Jorge. Something's come up. Rainbow is not available tomorrow."

Jenny plunged into thought as she thanked the pilot and hung up the phone. Why had Rainbow visited the sky diving company? Had she discovered something about Bella's death?

Chapter 20

"You have to come," Heather pleaded with Jenny. "Crystal especially wants you there."

"Look around, Heather," Jenny waved a hand at the crowded café. "People are lining up here thanks to Mandy and her Instagram. They want to book tables. There's no way I can get away."

Heather turned to Petunia.

"It's just a couple of hours. And it's at sunset. The café is closed by then."

"I don't mind," Petunia told her. "I can

take care of the prep for one day. Maybe Star can come and keep me company."

Heather went for the jugular.

"It's a chance to say goodbye to Rainbow."

Jenny couldn't say no to that.

A small group of people assembled at the Pelican Cove Country Club later that evening. The gazebo was covered in small bouquets of tulips and roses. Someone whispered they were Rainbow's favorite flowers. A priest had arrived from the mainland. In deference to Rainbow's wishes, no one wore black.

Crystal sniffled and Wayne looked

solemn. Kathy Mars dabbed at her eyes with a lace handkerchief. One of the girls gave a violin recital. Wayne asked if anyone wanted to say something. Almost all the girls had something nice to say about Rainbow.

"She's going to be missed," Heather whispered to Jenny.

Jenny's eyes misted over. She felt helpless. All her efforts had been futile. She wasn't any closer to finding out what happened, either to Bella or Rainbow.

"One of these people is a killer," she hissed at Heather. "Maybe it's one of these girls…just waiting to step into her role on the show."

"You think so?" Heather was skeptical.

"She was on to something," Jenny mumbled. "I'm sure about it."

The sun set over the ocean, painting the sky orange and mauve. Rainbow wasn't around to see it, but Jenny admitted she had been given a good farewell. Ray Fox caught her eye as they walked back to the club house.

"I didn't know you were coming."

"Rainbow and Bella were like sisters," he said. "Bella would have wanted me here."

"Do you think she would take her own life?"

"Never," Ray said, shaking his head. "She was ambitious. She had her kid to think about."

"So you believe she was murdered?"

Ray said nothing but his grim expression was answer enough.

Someone had ordered a sumptuous buffet of Rainbow's favorite dishes. Jenny guessed Wayne had something to do with it. He wasn't hiding his grief from anyone.

Jenny overheard the girls talking about the show. Everyone wanted to know who was going to replace Rainbow. The girls seemed excited but Jenny assumed that was natural. She peered at each of their faces as she bit into a slider. Had one of them deliberately poisoned Rainbow?

"Stop staring, Jenny!" Heather hissed in her ear. "Wayne wants to talk to you."

Wayne stood at one end of the long passage, gazing out at the dunes.

"I miss her," he told Jenny. "We were really close."

Wasn't he close to all the women in his life, Jenny mused. A sudden giggle erupted, making her feel mortified.

"I don't mean that way," Wayne clucked. "Rainbow was my best friend. We could talk for hours. She really knew me, you know. Knew Wayne Newman the person, not Wayne Newman the country music star."

"Shouldn't you have that with Crystal?"

Wayne shrugged.

"Crystal and I have an understanding.

Getting married now will give a big boost to our careers, and we both understand that."

"What if Crystal wasn't in the picture?" Jenny asked. "Would you have married Rainbow?"

Wayne hesitated. Then he shook his head.

"Rainbow didn't have that kind of fan base."

"But you did. Surely you could have elevated her career if you wanted to."

"It's too late now," Wayne shrugged.

"What's next for you, Wayne?"

"We are going back to Los Angeles in a

couple of days. We are shooting the pilot episode next week. We are all going to be pretty busy, I guess."

Kathy Mars spotted them from a distance and walked over.

"Thank you for coming," she told Jenny. "Rainbow would have wanted you here."

"When did you talk to her last?"

"Crystal and I were having tea out here. She seemed to be in a hurry."

"Was she going out?"

"She must be. She was twirling a set of car keys in her hand."

"Do you know when she got back?"

Kathy thought for a moment.

"She didn't turn up for dinner. I figured she must have met someone."

"But she didn't know anyone in town, did she?"

"Just Bella's husband," Kathy quipped.

Jenny tried to read Kathy's expression. Was she implying Ray Fox had harmed Rainbow?

"You must be looking forward to getting back home."

Kathy's handbag buzzed just as she opened her mouth to answer Jenny.

"Who's calling me now?" she muttered, struggling with the clasp.

"Let me help," Wayne said just then.

Kathy and Wayne both pulled at the bag at the same instant. The bag sprang open and its contents scattered on the floor.

"Look what you've done now!" Kathy exclaimed angrily.

Wayne bent down to pick everything up off the floor. A bottle of pills rolled down and came to rest by Jenny's foot.

She picked it up and quickly read the label before handing it back to Kathy.

"You're not sick, are you?" Heather asked solicitously.

"Oh no!" Kathy said, looking flustered. "Those are just my anxiety pills. Almost everyone in the business takes them. Right Wayne?"

"Huh?" Wayne asked.

Jenny couldn't wait to get away. She said goodbye and grabbed Heather's arm.

"What's the rush, Jenny?" Heather scowled, jerking her arm away.

"Did you see those pills?" Jenny asked as she backed out of the parking lot.

"Kathy's anxiety pills?"

"They can double as sleeping pills. I need to talk to Adam right now."

They rushed into the police station. Adam Hopkins stood at the front desk, ready to go home for the day.

"What's the matter now, Jenny?" he asked, correctly reading her expression. "Let's go into my office."

"What's the drug Rainbow took? Quick, tell me."

"We are waiting for a full tox screen," Adam told her patiently. "But if you must know, it was a cocktail of a popular anxiety drug mixed with something else."

"Aha!" Jenny banged her fist on the table.

She quickly told Adam about Kathy's pill bottle.

"It's a very common medicine, Jenny,"

Adam sighed. “Anybody could have a prescription for it.”

“But get this,” Jenny said with relish. “The bottle was almost empty.”

“We don’t know when the prescription was filled.”

“But you can find out?”

“I’ll look into it,” Adam promised. “But it may not be that easy,” he warned. “We will probably need a warrant.”

“Do what you think is best.”

Heather and Jenny lingered outside while Adam made a few calls. He came out just as they were saying goodbye to the desk clerk.

"How about going to Ethan's?" Adam asked. "I could use a bite to eat. I skipped lunch today."

Jenny looked at her watch reluctantly.

"Sorry. I'm meeting Jason in five minutes."

Adam turned around and walked to his car without a word.

"Did you have to blow him off?" Heather grumbled.

"I really have an appointment with Jason," Jenny stressed. "It's important."

"Are you just playing hard to get?"

"No, Heather! I need to talk to Jason about a business matter."

Jenny crossed the street and walked two doors down to Jason's office.

"Come on in," he called out to her.

Jenny grabbed a soda from the small refrigerator in Jason's office. She sat down heavily and took a few sips of the cold drink.

"What do you have for me?"

"It looks tough."

"Do I have enough funds in my account? That's all I want to know."

"You do, Jenny. But if you spend this, you won't have a cushion until next year. You'll have barely enough for any incidental expenses."

"I don't need much," she shrugged. "Living in Pelican Cove is really cheap."

"What about Nick's college fees?"

"His father is paying those. They don't come out of my account."

"I still wouldn't advise it, Jenny."

"Is it going to solve our problems?"

"You know there will always be something else."

"Of course, but I am just talking about the contest. I love this town, Jason. And if there's even a slight chance we could be the Prettiest Town in America, I don't want to stand in the way."

"How do you know Petunia wants this?"

"Are you kidding? She's lived here almost all her life. She wants to win too."

"So when are you giving her the good news?"

"I'm not," Jenny said. "You are."

"How do you mean?"

"The Boardwalk Café is going to get a silent partner. It will be just enough to cover the cost of refurbishment."

"Jenny, you're investing almost a year's income in this. Are you sure you don't want credit for it?"

"I'm sure, Jason. I have to work side by side with Petunia every day. I don't want her to feel beholden to me."

"Jenny King," Jason said, his eyes shining with admiration. "You're something else."

"Stop flattering me," Jenny blushed, slapping Jason on the arm. "Now what about that other matter?"

"I have good news," Jason exulted. "Our offer has been accepted."

Jenny felt her heart speed up.

"What does that mean?" she asked, leaning forward in her seat.

"We are in escrow, Jenny!"

"We are?"

"You are now the owner of a charming sea facing three storied Victorian."

"Seaview," Jenny whispered lovingly. "Is it really mine?"

"Congratulations, Jenny! This is a big leap for you. You are a home owner in Pelican Cove."

"It's like a dream come true."

"Who do you want to tell first?"

"I'm calling Nick," Jenny said, laughing and crying at the same time.

She fished her cell phone out of her purse and waved it around for a signal. Jason picked up his desk phone and placed it in front of Jenny.

"Call him from this. I can add it to your bill."

They both laughed at that.

Jenny spent the next few minutes talking to her son while Jason looked on indulgently.

"What about fixing up Seaview?" Jenny asked after she hung up. "Do I have to wait until next year?"

"I already factored it in," Jason told her. "You have a nice chunk of money set aside for repairs at Seaview."

"Oh Jason, I am so happy!"

"Ready to share the news with

everyone?"

"You remember our promise?" she asked Jason. "No one can know about my involvement in the café. No one."

"I'm your lawyer, Jenny. You can trust me with your life."

He took her hand and kissed it gently.

"You can trust me, period."

Jenny sprang up and danced a little jig. She couldn't have imagined this outcome in her wildest dreams. Just a few months ago, she had come to Pelican Cove with just the clothes on her back. A good divorce lawyer had made sure her cheating husband treated her fairly. It was the least she deserved after twenty years of marriage.

"Let's go out and celebrate," Jason said. "There's this great seafood place on the boardwalk at Virginia Beach. They have oysters on the half shell and wood fire grilled fish."

"Can I change first?" Jenny asked. "We can take Star with us, can't we?"

"Of course we can," Jason smiled. "What's a celebration without family?"

Chapter 21

Jenny chatted with Captain Charlie early the next morning. The old salt had appeared on the steps of the Boardwalk Café at 6 AM sharp.

"How about a hot scone?" he asked. "Petunia's been talking them up a lot."

"Coming right up," Jenny smiled. "I made strawberry jam to go with them."

The phone rang at 8 AM. Petunia's face broke into a big smile after she answered it. Jenny acted surprised.

"Someone wants to invest in the café,"

Petunia said, her eyes saucer like in wonder. "He's ready to pay for all the repairs the town committee wants us to do."

"That's great news," Jenny said, giving her a hug. "You said yes, right?"

"Of course I did. Beggars can't be choosers."

"You're not a beggar, Petunia. The Boardwalk Café is a landmark. Any investor should be proud to invest in such a well loved place."

"All that is fine, dear, but anyone who's putting up a big chunk of money is entitled to think what they want."

"When do we meet this Santa Claus?"

Petunia's expression said she wasn't too happy with Jenny's flippant tone.

"We don't. That's the condition."

"Doesn't matter to us," Jenny shrugged. "Why don't you call Barb and Mandy and rub it in their face?"

"What's got into you, Jenny?" Petunia groaned but she giggled like a naughty girl.

"Call the contractor too while you're at it."

"One thing at a time," Petunia said, pressing the buttons on the phone.

"Hola!" a deep voice came from the counter.

Jenny spotted Ray Fox standing there with a duffel bag slung over his shoulder.

“Good Morning, Ray. You’re out early today.”

“I came to say bye,” he said. “I want to thank you for all your help.”

“I didn’t really do anything,” Jenny said bitterly.

Her failure to find Bella’s killer still rankled.

“You did your best,” Ray Fox said with a shrug. “I guess we will never know what happened to my Bella.”

“Where are you off to?”

"Back home. I'm taking Bella with me."

"So the police cleared you, I guess."

"I can't stay here indefinitely. Jason talked to them. They don't have any evidence against me so they have to let me go."

"When's your flight?"

"I'm flying out from Norfolk later today. But I want to get a head start. I can't wait to get out of here."

"I can understand," Jenny nodded gloomily.

She wrapped a hot scone for him and poured coffee into a travel container.

"It's on the house."

Ray gave her an awkward hug. He was gone soon after that.

Petunia came out looking relieved.

"The contractor can start work today. We should be able to meet the town's deadline by a whisker."

The kitchen phone rang again and Jenny rushed inside to answer it.

"We're going shopping!" Heather screamed over the phone. "I'm picking you up in five minutes, Jenny. Get ready."

"You know I can't leave the café…" Jenny objected. "What's the rush?"

"Just be there, Jenny. We can talk on the way."

A black stretch limo pulled up outside the café five minutes later. Heather's head sprang up through the sun roof. She waved madly at Jenny, urging her to hurry.

"I think you better go, dear," Petunia laughed. "Don't worry about the café."

A uniformed chauffer stepped out of the car and came around to the passenger side. He held the door open for Jenny. Jenny snatched her bag and ran down the stairs, unable to curb her excitement.

Crystal and Heather reclined against the plush seats, sipping glasses of champagne.

"What's going on?"

"Just get in," Heather urged. "We are shopping for Crystal's wedding dress."

"I'm getting married tomorrow," Crystal preened, looking as cool as a cucumber.

"But I thought you were all leaving this weekend."

"Tomorrow is our last day in town," Crystal explained. "What better way to end this horrible trip?"

"Wayne's going along with it then?"

"Of course he is," Crystal told Jenny. "He proposed to me again last night. The studio's thrilled. They are going to film everything this time and use it for the show."

"Wow!" Jenny exclaimed, giving Heather a questioning look.

"Only bummer is, we just have one day to shop for the wedding."

"Aren't you wearing your Vera Wang?"

Crystal's body quivered.

"That dress is jinxed. I'm getting something new from a local designer."

Jenny was honest.

"I don't think you can have a custom-made dress in a day, Crystal."

"Throw enough money and you can get anything," Crystal dismissed. "Mom's already booked appointments for us with the area's top designers. We can give them credit on the show. None of them is going to pass up this opportunity."

"Crystal changed her wedding colors," Heather enthused. "All the bridesmaids get new dresses too. I've got everyone's measurements right here."

"Where are all the other girls?" Jenny asked, noticing their absence.

"They are at the spa," Crystal told them. "Everyone's panicking because they are going on camera tomorrow."

Jenny wondered why Crystal wasn't at the spa too. But she kept her thoughts to herself.

"So I can get a dress that fits this time," she joked.

"Why don't you relax?" Crystal invited. "Sip some champagne. It's Moe Chandon, compliments of the studio."

"Don't mind if I do," Jenny giggled nervously.

Jenny had spent her life attending parties where the finest French champagnes flowed like water. But she had missed them since coming to Pelican Cove.

"What's our first stop?"

"Williamsburg," Heather supplied. "Crystal wanted to go to Richmond but I talked her out of it. It's too far."

"Are we going to the outlets?" Jenny asked eagerly, already planning to squeeze in some discount shopping.

"Outlets?" Crystal asked, looking horrified. "We are not shopping retail, Jenny. Surely you know that."

Jenny began feeling light-headed after an hour of sipping champagne. Heather pulled out some cheese and crackers from a picnic hamper. There was a jar of olive tapenade and a loaf of crusty bread. The girls feasted on them. Crystal refused to eat anything.

They spent a couple of hours in Williamsburg, visiting four different designers. Crystal tried on exactly one wedding gown at each place. Jenny thought she looked gorgeous in every one of them, but Crystal rejected them all.

"Can we stop for lunch?" Heather asked.

"We can eat in the car," Crystal told them. "I ordered Chinese food."

The car sped north toward Hampton Roads while the girls feasted on the greasy salty food.

Crystal tried on two more wedding gowns. She fumed when a designer showed her a mermaid design.

"This is so last year!"

Their next stop was on the outskirts of Virginia Beach. Thankfully, Crystal fell in love with the gown. It came with black gloves and a big bow at the back. Crystal announced it was suitably 'au courant'.

The bridesmaids got dresses in pale blue.

"Wayne's meeting us for dinner in Virginia Beach," Crystal announced, reading a text from her phone. "We are going to this fancy seafood place on the boardwalk."

"I've been there with Jason," Jenny told them. "It's really fancy."

"As fancy as this place can get, I suppose," Crystal quipped.

Wayne was already at their table when they reached the restaurant. They ordered a tower of seafood, with oysters, crab legs and jumbo shrimp. Crab cakes followed, with grilled fish and seared scallops.

"Have you ordered the whole menu, Wayne?" Jenny asked him.

She dipped a giant shrimp into cocktail sauce and exclaimed as she was about to bite into it.

"What's he doing here?"

Jenny had spotted someone who looked like Ray Fox. She stood up and walked over to the table. She had guessed right.

"You're still here?" she burst out.

"My flight was delayed," he told her. "Someone recommended this restaurant so I took a cab and came here."

Jenny thought it was a long way to travel just for some seafood.

"All the way from Norfolk?"

"I have nothing else to do," Ray shrugged. "I'm glad I came. This place is really something, huh?"

Jenny went back to her table after that. Crystal and Wayne were arguing about Jordan almonds. Crystal wanted a mix of white and pale blue nuts to match her wedding colors. Wayne didn't know what the fuss was about.

"I know a shop here that sells them," Heather said eagerly. "Why don't we go check it out, Crystal? They do bulk orders. You can get a few pounds for tomorrow."

Crystal agreed immediately. They decided to walk to the store to work off their meal.

Atlantic Avenue was crowded, with

tourists jostling each other for space. Jenny and Heather walked arm in arm, followed by Wayne and Crystal. Wayne was talking about how he had liked the multicolored Jordan almonds as a kid. They stopped to cross the street as the light turned red.

Jenny suddenly felt her knees buckle as she fell into the oncoming traffic. She landed on her side as horns blared and a large SUV screeched to a stop barely inches from her face. Jenny felt the ground spin as she blacked out momentarily.

The next thing she knew, she was sitting on a small stool on the sidewalk. Heather and Wayne were fawning over her, asking if she was hurt. Crystal stood a few feet away, looking at her in disgust.

"You're bleeding!" Heather exclaimed as she noticed Jenny's dress. The right side of her body was soaked in blood.

Wayne pulled out a handkerchief and started dabbing her arm with it. One of the onlookers handed over a bottle of water. Wayne washed her hand and gently wiped the blood off.

"I think it's just a flesh wound," he said. "You must have cut your arm on something."

Jenny felt a searing pain in her shoulder. Her arm didn't respond when she tried to raise it.

"Looks like you dislocated your shoulder," another guy on the sidewalk offered. "There's an urgent care place a couple of miles out. You should get yourself checked out."

"Let's just go home," Jenny pleaded.

Wayne would have none of it. They took her to the 24 hour clinic. The man on the street had been right about Jenny's shoulder. The doctor popped it back in place and gave her a sling to wear. She had a few more scratches and one big cut on her arm. She had to get a tetanus shot because she didn't remember when she had her last one.

The limo sped home over the Chesapeake Bay and crossed the bridge leading to Pelican Cove.

"I'm so sorry about all this," Wayne apologized as he helped Jenny out of the car.

Crystal had dozed off, probably piqued by all the attention Jenny was getting.

There were a few figures sitting out on Star's porch.

"Jenny!"

Three different voices cried out in the night.

Jenny looked up to see Adam and Jason standing on either side of her aunt.

"What are you doing here?"

"Adam wanted to ask you out for a walk," Star explained. "Jason brought dinner."

"What happened, Jenny?" Adam

demanded curtly. "Are you hurt?"

"How did this happen?" Jason asked sharply.

Jenny gave them the Cliff Notes version.

"It's getting late," she said meaningfully, tipping her head at Wayne.

Jason thanked Wayne and accepted his impromptu wedding invitation.

Adam opened his mouth as soon as the limo went out of sight. Jason stopped him.

"Let's get her settled in."

"I'm fine," Jenny stressed. "It's just a

few cuts and bruises…"

"And a dislocated shoulder," Star guessed.

"Think carefully, Jenny," Adam said after she was ensconced in an armchair inside the cottage.

Star had pressed a steaming mug of tea in her hand and covered her with a soft rug.

"Tell me exactly what happened."

"I don't know. We were standing on the sidewalk, waiting to cross the road. I must have lost my balance."

"Or someone pushed you," Jason said bluntly.

"Where was Wayne Newman when this happened?" Adam asked grimly.

"He was right behind me."

Chapter 22

Jenny's bridesmaid's dress fit her properly this time. The blue sling on her arm matched her dress.

Star got all choked up as she looked at her. She had come to drop Jenny off at the country club.

"You look beautiful, sweetie."

Jenny held up her arm.

"I'm going to be an eyesore. They will probably keep me out of the wedding photos."

Star gave Jenny a meaningful look.

"Are you sure you want to go to this shindig? We can just turn around and drive home, you know."

"I need to be there," Jenny stressed. "This is my last chance to get a close look at these people. I'm sure one of them is the murderer."

"You'll be careful, won't you?" Star frowned.

"Don't worry about me, Auntie."

Star looked down at her paint spattered smock. She would have crashed the wedding party if she was wearing something decent.

"Jason's going to meet you here?"

"Yes, he's my date."

Star pulled up in the club's porte-cochere. Jason was waiting for them. He helped Jenny out of the car and escorted her up the steps.

Heather and Chris Williams were seated in the lounge, sipping slim flutes of champagne. Heather came around to hug Jenny.

"So what's the plan?" Jenny asked.

"The studio people are setting up on the lawn," Heather reported. "It's going to be a fairy-tale wedding, Jenny."

Jenny and Heather discussed wedding details like flowers and arches and dresses. Jason and Chris pretended they were bored. One of Crystal's posse came in and began rounding everyone up.

Jenny spotted the wedding arch from a distance. A big white tent was erected at one side for the reception. The color theme of white and yellow was reflected everywhere. A bunch of ushers began leading people to their seats. Jason and Chris chose a couple of chairs in the back row.

A lot of studio staff was milling around, dressed in black. A man sat in a crane forty feet high, fiddling with a large camera. The crane swept across the landscape, recording the activities of the guests.

A couple of tight lipped men wearing tuxedos stood at one side, observing everything with eagle-like precision.

"They are the big bosses," Heather whispered. "The show's producers."

The bridesmaids huddled together in a group, dressed in blue like Heather and Jenny. One of the girls came over and told Jenny the studio wanted her to stand aside.

"It's your sling," she said apologetically. "It won't look good on film."

"No problem," Jenny shrugged.

"Where's the groom?" Jenny mumbled to herself.

A whir sounded just then and a plane came into view.

"Are you kidding me?" Jenny burst out.

All the assembled guests trained their eyes toward the plane. Some of them were clutching each other's hands. A body dropped from the plane followed by another. The two bodies plummeted to the ground, gaining speed rapidly until their fall was thwarted mid-air. A canopy unfurled over each body and they began drifting to the ground.

Jenny heard the crane whir as the camera captured the spectacle.

A cheer went up through the crowd as the two bodies landed on the ground with a soft thud. Wayne stood up first and pulled off his parachute. He was dressed in a tuxedo, wearing a white rose in his lapel. He turned around and helped Crystal out of her chute.

"Wasn't Crystal deathly afraid of

heights?" Jenny asked Heather urgently. "She said she wouldn't jump from a plane for all the money in the world."

One of the studio execs overheard them. He leaned toward Jenny with a smirk on his face.

"All the money in the world turned out to be a million dollars in this case. They all have their price."

"I just hope she's worth it," the other guy in the suit said.

The first studio exec looked up toward the guy on the crane. He gave them a thumbs up sign.

"After that dive, I say she's worth every penny."

"Aren't you glad we sent her for that certification course?"

"What course?" Jenny asked urgently, grabbing one of the men by his arm.

"The sky diving certification of course!" he said, raising an eyebrow at her arm.

"So Crystal has knowledge of sky diving?"

"How do you think she did a solo dive?" one of the studio execs asked. "She can't do that without being a certified diver."

"She must know all about parachutes and stuff."

The other studio exec butted in.

"I'm a C level diver. Even the most basic level requires you to know all about your equipment."

"You're sure about all this, right?" Jenny asked.

"Of course we are," the guys chorused. "We are very particular about licensing requirements. There's no way we will let an actor do something without the proper permissions."

The strains of the wedding march sounded. Kathy Mars stood ready to walk Crystal down the aisle. Wayne stood at the other end, an inscrutable expression on his face. One of the studio minions held up a big sign saying 'smile' and waved it in front of Wayne. Wayne's lips stretched in a ghastly smile. Then his eyes crinkled at the edges and the smile almost looked real.

"Stop!" Jenny roared. "Stop this wedding."

Everyone stared at her as if she was a mad woman.

"Stop this wedding now, Wayne, or you will regret it."

Jenny elbowed Crystal and walked down the aisle toward Wayne. She whispered something in his ear. Wayne pulled a phone out of his pocket and pressed some buttons.

"What is this crap?" one of the studio execs thundered. "Who is that woman?"

Sirens split the sky as the crowd began

to murmur.

Crystal flung her bouquet aside with a cry and plowed into Jenny. Before she realized what was happening, Jenny found herself flat on the ground with Crystal sitting on top of her.

"You couldn't heed my warning, could you?"

Several pairs of hands rushed to pull her off Jenny. Jenny doubled up in pain as Crystal punched her ailing shoulder.

A couple of cars with lights flashing drove up on the grass and stopped right next to Crystal. Adam Hopkins leapt out of one of them.

"Stop running, Crystal," Jenny said, struggling to get up from the floor.

"We know you did it. You killed Bella and Rainbow."

Crystal let out an inhuman shriek.

"Yes!" she screamed. "I killed them both. And I almost got away with it too."

"Are you getting this?" one of the studio execs whispered in a walkie-talkie.

"Why did you do it, Crystal?" Wayne asked. "Do you know you killed my baby too?"

"That's why she had to go, of course," Crystal said, laughing hysterically. "I didn't want to be saddled with someone else's brat."

"Bella and Ray were going to raise the child as their own."

"You expect me to believe that?" Crystal leered. "You were seeing Bella behind my back. You think I didn't know, did you? Everyone knew, Wayne. The whole world knew. You made a laughing stock out of me."

"You didn't have to marry him," Jenny pointed out.

"Of course I had to marry him," Crystal cried. "I had to marry some idiot. He was as good as any other."

"How did you do it, Crystal?" Adam asked. "Did you slash Bella's parachute yourself?"

"It was all meticulously planned,"

Crystal boasted. "My mother paid Rainbow to get Bella thrown off the set. I knew Rainbow felt guilty about it. I told her the show was doing a special segment. Two brides would turn up for Wayne Newman's wedding. But he would choose just one of them. I told her the studio wanted to bring Bella back on the show. And this was going to be her entry vehicle."

"Rainbow bought that?"

"She bought it hook, line and sinker," Crystal laughed. "Rainbow took details of my wedding dress and ordered the exact same one. It was going to be Bella's 'something borrowed' item. The sapphire was her 'something blue'."

"What about the parachute?" Jenny asked. "Bella was an experienced diver.

How did she go up without checking her rig?"

"I told them it was specially provided by the studio. It had the show's name painted on it. Or some such crap. They swallowed it without question."

"So Bella went up wearing that chute, thinking she was doing it for the cameras?"

Crystal nodded. "Imagine the look on her face when the chute didn't open!"

"Didn't Rainbow suspect you after Bella died?" Jenny asked.

"I threatened to have her fired. What would happen to her poor kid then?"

"Did Rainbow try to blackmail you

later?"

"If only… I could have thrown some money at her. But she developed a conscience. I followed her out to the airfield, saw her talking to that pilot. That's when I knew she had to go."

"How did you kill Rainbow?" Adam asked her.

"I knew she carried that metal water bottle everywhere she went. Some crap about saving the environment…I ground some of her sleeping pills and my mom's anxiety pills and put them in the steel bottle."

"Did you ask her to drink that water?"

Crystal laughed again.

"I gave her some pain pills when she complained about a headache. Told her to wash them down with plenty of water. She drank the whole bottle. Said she was thirsty from being out in the sun."

"Why did you do it, Crystal?" Jenny asked. "You were already the star of the show. What did Bella ever do to you?"

"She was going to steal Wayne away from me," Crystal howled. "I couldn't let that happen."

She looked at Kathy Mars, a bewildered expression on her face.

"Could I, Mom?"

"If Wayne was cheating on you, wouldn't it have been easier to just dump him and find a new guy?"

"I'm going to be Mrs. Wayne Newman," Crystal whined. "It's already scripted."

Adam and his officers took Crystal away. Jason and Chris whisked Jenny and Heather away from the club as soon as possible.

"Are you feeling alright?" Heather asked her worriedly. "We need to take you to the doctor again."

"I'm fine. I just need to ask Wayne something."

Wayne came over when Jenny beckoned him.

"Did you really not know Bella was on

that plane with you?”

“I swear, Jenny, I had no idea. I was thinking about our baby. I was hoping Ray and Bella would let me see him now and then.”

Jason’s eyes gleamed as he stared at Jenny.

“You did it again! You’re one amazing woman, Jenny King.”

Epilogue

The Boardwalk Café looked brand spanking new. The contractors had finished the renovations in record time. Other Main Street businesses had done their bit and Mandy James had accomplished the job she had been hired for.

Small blue plaques proclaiming Pelican Cove to be the Prettiest Town in America hung over every lamp post on Main Street. Flowers bloomed in window boxes and small flower beds. Colorful bikes were lined up against the café, inviting locals and tourists alike to pedal down the boardwalk and enjoy the beauty.

The Magnolias were assembled on the deck of the café. Petunia had graciously invited Barb and Mandy too. The other café regulars were all present. Jason, Adam, Chris and Captain Charlie sipped sweet tea from tall glasses and talked about some football game. Jimmy Parsons walked up the steps shyly, looking freshly showered, wearing a clean shirt.

Jenny greeted him warmly and led him toward the guys. Jenny's son Nick chatted with Adam's twin girls. They were spending the rest of the summer in Pelican Cove.

Mandy was leaving town in a few days so everyone was gathered for an informal farewell party for her.

"Let's eat," Jenny announced, bringing out a big tray loaded with plates and bowls brimming with food.

Heather and Molly followed with another tray.

"This barbecue sauce is super, Mom," Nick declared, licking his fingers as he bit into some juicy chicken.

"You're a good cook, Petunia," Captain Charlie winked, "but Jenny here has you beat. Got any more specials coming up?"

"Something with blueberries, maybe?" Jenny grinned. "Wait and see."

The party proceeded merrily and everyone declared they had eaten too much.

"Asher Cohen's centennial is coming up," Betty Sue Morse reminded the group. "Too bad you won't be here to plan it, Mandy. We could have used your help."

After the town won the award, Betty Sue had decided Mandy was the best thing that ever happened to Pelican Cove.

"There's a 100 year old man in Pelican Cove?" Mandy asked, wide eyed.

"Sure is," Petunia nodded. "We are planning a big party for him. Star is in charge of the Centennial Committee."

"You should bake a special cake for the occasion, Jenny," Betty Sue declared.

Adam sidled close to Jenny and pulled her aside.

"What are you doing tomorrow night?"

"Let me check my calendar," Jenny joked.

Her eyes twinkled as she looked up at Adam.

"Were you thinking of asking me out, Sheriff?"

The twins and Nick stole glances at them, giggling at some secret joke.

"Yes, Jenny King. I am asking you out on a date. A proper date."

Jenny placed a hand on Adam's arm and leaned forward to whisper in his ear.

"I thought you'd never ask."

THE END

Thank you for reading this book. If you enjoyed this book, please consider leaving a brief review here. Even a few words or a line or two will do.

As an indie author, I rely on reviews to spread the word about my book. Your assistance will be very helpful and greatly appreciated.

I would also really appreciate it if you tell your friends and family about the book. Word of mouth is an author's best friend, and it will be of immense help to me.

Many Thanks!

Author Leena Clover

http://leenaclover.com

Leenaclover@gmail.com

http://twitter.com/leenaclover

https://www.facebook.com/leenaclovercozymysterybooks

Other books by Leena Clover

Pelican Cove Cozy Mystery Series -

Strawberries and Strangers

Berries and Birthdays

Sprinkles and Skeletons

Waffles and Weekends

Muffins and Mobsters

Parfaits and Paramours

Truffles and Troubadours

Sundaes and Sinners

Croissants and Cruises

Dolphin Bay Cozy Mystery Series

Raspberry Chocolate Murder

Orange Thyme Death

Apple Caramel Mayhem

Cranberry Sage Miracle

Meera Patel Cozy Mystery Series -

Gone with the Wings

A Pocket Full of Pie

For a Few Dumplings More

Back to the Fajitas

Christmas with the Franks

Join my Newsletter

Get access to exclusive bonus content, sneak peeks, giveaways and much more. Also get a chance to join my exclusive ARC group, the people who get first dibs on all my new books.

Sign up at the following link and join the fun.

Click here → **http://www.subscribepage.com/leenaclovernl**

I love to hear from my readers, so please feel free to connect with me at any of the following places.

Website – **http://leenaclover.com**

Twitter – https://twitter.com/leenaclover

Facebook – http://facebook.com/leenacloverc ozymysterybooks

Instagram – http://instagram.com/leenaclover

Email – leenaclover@gmail.com

Made in the USA
Coppell, TX
25 November 2021